"You don't get what you want very often, do you, Princess?" Carter asked softly.

Sophie gave a small, almost imperceptible shake of her head.

"That's what I thought," he murmured, and cupped her face with both hands.

It's just a kiss, he told himself, lowering his head to hers. *Just a kiss to take away that lonely look from her eyes.* But that was before he felt the softness of her mouth beneath his and breathed in her small sigh.

The quick heat darting through him demanded that he kiss her more deeply, pull her taut little body into his arms, know the feel of her small breasts against his chest. She would fit perfectly there. She would fit perfectly everywhere.

With his body demanding more, but his mind telling him he'd already done more than he should, his hands drifted from her face. "That *wasn't* because you're a princess...."

Dear Reader,

What could a hard-driving, hard-riding, some say hard-*headed* Montana cattle rancher possibly have in common with a cultured, tea-drinking, temporarily-banished European princess? That was the question I asked myself when Sophie and Carter's story first started brewing.

Then I thought about my husband.

On the surface, we didn't seem to have much in common, either. His family was small, calm and lived 100 miles from a town with stoplights. My family was big, chaotic and about twenty minutes from a city of nearly 200,000. He was (and still is) gregarious, spontaneous, organized, practical and athletic. I was (and am) so…not.

But the heart has a way of looking past the obvious and finding what matters. We did. And so did Carter and Sophie. Like us, it just took them a while to discover how much they truly shared.

Here's to your discoveries!

Christine Flynn

THE RANCHER & THE
RELUCTANT PRINCESS

CHRISTINE FLYNN

Silhouette®
SPECIAL EDITION®
Published by Silhouette Books
America's Publisher of Contemporary Romance

SILHOUETTE BOOKS

ISBN-13: 978-0-373-65449-9
ISBN-10:   0-373-65449-9

Recycling programs for this product may not exist in your area.

THE RANCHER & THE RELUCTANT PRINCESS

Visit Silhouette Books at www.eHarlequin.com

Printed in U.S.A.

Books by Christine Flynn

Silhouette Special Edition

Silhouette Books

CHRISTINE FLYNN

admits to being interested in just about everything, which is why she considers herself fortunate to have turned her interest in writing into a career. She feels that a writer gets to explore it all and, to her, exploring relationships—especially the intense, bittersweet or even lighthearted relationships between men and women—is fascinating.

Chapter One

Sophie Saxe-Savoyard had messed up. Royally.

Granted, she'd been preoccupied—and tired, actually, of giving yet another version of the same scripted "For the Glory of Queen and Country" speech she'd delivered at heaven only knew how many other ribbon-cutting ceremonies. Still, that didn't excuse what she'd done.

With that painful little detail nagging at her, she listened to the engines of her small private jet change pitch as it touched down. She knew she should have simply bitten her tongue, smiled and offered something Royal Press Office approved. It was just that the frustration she usually buried at having to keep her personal opinions to herself had apparently leaked past her guard when the sole reporter present had asked the same inane questions about how it felt to see yet another garden planted in a traffic circle. It hadn't occurred to her, however, that the honest comment that had slipped out, about failing to see the need to replace perfectly lovely Valdovian flower bulbs with the less vibrant imported ones, would get her called onto the carpet.

That particular carpet had been the antique Aubusson in the drawing room of her grandmother, the Queen of Valdovia. Her Majesty had promptly informed her that the bulbs had been a gift from Luzandria last year and that Sophie's comment had insulted the Luzandrian ambassador and nearly destroyed what apparently were extremely delicate and lucrative trade negotiations between Valdovia and the other small, European nation.

Sophie hadn't been told beforehand that they were a gift. She hadn't even known the countries were in negotiations. Unlike her mother, the Crown Princess, and her older brother, Prince Nathaniel, who would someday be Prince Royal, as far down the line of succession as she was with four siblings and their children ahead of her, she wasn't privy to matters of national importance, or their details. Her job was to fill in at events not deemed important enough for those higher up the royal food chain.

Her appearance at those events, however, had been cancelled. Specifically, the opening of an equestrian park, standing in as a royal substitute for one of her sisters at an arts luncheon and her weekly reading at the Royal Library for Children. The Queen had regally accepted Sophie's sincere apology, but she'd also ordered her out of public view. The Royal Press Office had received no fewer than a dozen requests for interviews with her from European media since learning of the ambassador's snit and it was deemed best that she avoid microphones for a while. Especially since the press had dug up a few of her less recent gaffes and were reminding the public all over again of her unfortunate taste in suitors. Her grandmother's advisors had thought it best that Sophie go where she couldn't be trapped by a reporter into compromising herself, or saying something else that might jeopardize the nation's economy. All had agreed that somewhere off the continent would be best—which was why she'd just landed on a dirt runway in what appeared to be the Middle-of-Nowhere, Montana, USA.

Her American uncle's uniformed pilot emerged from the cockpit. The copilot rose to retrieve her luggage. Both men, equally trusted, had apparently been in her uncle's employ for years.

"There's Mr. Mabry's place." The gray-haired pilot nodded at the view visible through the small oval window beside her. "On that rise."

The leaden sky threatened rain. Beneath those heavy clouds, spring-green prairie stretched toward jagged, snow-capped mountains. The sole structure visible, a spectacular glass and log lodge in the distance, belonged to Sophie's Aunt Brianna and Uncle Matthew Mabry. Aunt Bree, her mother's younger sister, had caused a bit of a stir herself when she'd broken her engagement to a duke and married the rich, now-retired American actor-turned-philanthropist. Her aunt had warned her that their summer lodge was quite remote, and that the amenities and staff were not what she was accustomed to at the royal palace in Valdovia.

As hemmed in and controlled as Sophie had felt lately, she had assured her aunt that she didn't mind being banished to Montana's legendary, wide-open spaces. What she hadn't said was how relieved she was to be away from the palace's oppressive formality for a while. There was something almost stifling about having people scramble to do things for her that she could easily do herself.

It occurred to her, vaguely, that she wouldn't mind

fleeing her life in general when she noticed a silver-gray, bull-nosed pickup truck bounce along the dirt road toward the private airstrip.

"That," the pilot announced, with a nod for the driver's punctuality, "should be your ride."

Thoughts of escape surfaced once more as she thanked both men for their assistance and insisted politely that she could manage the bags herself. The notion of permanent liberation had been dismissed, however, by the time she descended the short flight of stairs with a suitcase in each hand and her oversized purse slung over her shoulder.

She felt utterly certain that her dissatisfaction existed only because of her mortification over having embarrassed her grandmother, her mother and her country. Her present situation excluded, she didn't doubt that she would live within the same narrow parameters in the future as she had in the past.

Reaching the ground, she popped up the bags' handles and pulled them toward the waiting truck. As she did, a chill breeze whipped the ends of her dark, low ponytail against her cheek. She let the wind push them back, resignation in her every step. When she was summoned, she'd go home, dutifully stick to "correct" responses when in public—and probably in private, just to be safe—and ultimately settle into the dutiful sort of marriage her parents had existed in for forty years. It wasn't that she didn't want to marry. She just wanted a man who loved *her,* not her title or royal bloodlines. Because of who she was, though, she would never know if it was her or her connections anyone cared about. At least by marrying one of the dukes or princes on the royal short list, both would know the match took advantage of neither party.

She'd just admitted she'd give anything to know just *once*

what it would be like to live like a normal, almost twenty-nine-year-old woman whose blood would matter only if it needed to be typed for transfusion when she lifted her head.

Her steps faltered.

Aunt Bree had told her she would be met by the caretaker of their retreat, an older gentleman of average height and build with gray hair by the name of Dave Bauer. But the six-feet, four inches of muscle and testosterone in denim and a heavy oilskin jacket climbing from the truck couldn't possibly be that man. There was nothing average—or old—about him. Not the width of his shoulders, the rugged features below the curled brim of his cowboy hat or the long-legged stride that carried him to a halt in front of her.

Blocking her view of everything but the heavy fabric covering his impossibly broad chest, he gave a quick tug on his hat's brim.

"Mornin', miss."

At the deep, smoky rumble of his voice, her focus jerked up. The shadow of a beard lingered on his recently shaved face. A small scar hooked from the corner of his carved, decidedly sensual mouth.

Unreadable gray eyes shot with shards of silver moved from hers to graze the length of her body. That jarringly thorough appraisal lasted barely long enough for her to draw a breath of the clean, damp air. Yet, he left her feeling as if he'd just dismissed her as being of no particular interest at all as he reached out his big, work-roughened hand.

Years of breeding masked hesitation as she extended her own hand, palm down, prepared to accept his grasp and bow.

"This all you have?" he asked, grabbing the bags she'd released.

He wanted her luggage.

Disconcerted by his lack of response to her automatic, courtly formality, feeling oddly awkward, she curled her fingers into her palm.

"It is."

"Let's go then."

Uncertainty kept her where she was. The rich and royal—even those of little significance—were raised to be aware of their personal security. When arrangements changed without notice, little red flags went up. "But you're not Mr. Bauer."

"The name's Carter McLeod."

"I was expecting Mr. Bauer."

"I'm aware of that, miss," he told her, sounding as if he wished she'd hurry up. "But Dave couldn't make it. His wife asked me to meet your plane."

Carter glanced toward the small jet on the runway he shared with the Mabrys, nodded to the pilot he'd helped with a fuel-line problem last year. Recognizing him as a friend of his employer, the pilot waved back and pulled up the flight stairs.

Carter's attention swung back to his passenger. He couldn't tell if he'd heard accusation in her voice, or something more like disquiet. He caught an accent, though. Something light on *R*s and long on vowels.

In too much of a hurry to wonder about it, he looked from the narrow black slacks and gray tweed jacket covering her slender frame, then motioned to the large, utilitarian vehicle parked beyond the airstrip. "If this is all you've got, go on and get in." He lifted his chin toward the sky. "Those clouds are about ready to open up."

Leaving her to follow, Carter headed across hard-packed earth with his passenger's designer luggage in hand. Personally, he saw no point in advertising other people's brands. To his way of thinking a brand should identify what belonged to a person; cattle, equipment. Relying on someone else's initials to make a statement seemed to impress certain other people, though. He didn't get it, but his ex-wife definitely had.

Scowling at the reminder of his not-so-distant past, he stowed the luggage in the crew-cab. The door closed on the unwelcome thought with the crisp report of a gun shot.

The woman hadn't budged. She stood right where he'd left her, twenty feet away, her hands clasped loosely in front of her. His inclination was to holler at her to hurry up, but it wasn't his habit to be rude. Not deliberately, anyway.

Her long, shiny brown ponytail swayed as she warily checked to make sure the plane hadn't moved.

Jenny Bauer's call to him had been quick and urgent. She hadn't told him who this woman was, other than that she was a guest of the Mabrys. As preoccupied and upset as she'd been, Jenny had been sparing of details on all fronts.

He truly didn't have time for this.

With a mental sigh, he headed across the ground he'd just covered. This particular guest of the Mabrys didn't strike him as being one of the glitterati in Matthew's illustrious inner circle. Not that Carter knew many of those guests. He'd only met a few who'd managed to mistake a cow path for a bridle trail and wound up at the Mother Lode's compound needing directions back. He really only knew Matt. And, then, only as a man he respected for what the retired actor had done to keep development from encroaching on Carter's own 32,000-acre spread. Unlike some of his employees, he had no interest at all in the privileged lives of the rich and famous and paid little attention to the flutter and buzz in town when the Mabrys or their guests were around. All he knew from what he'd overheard was that the majority of women who arrived there tended to be beautiful, sophisticated and stylish—and that they always arrived with staff.

This woman was stylish, he supposed, though sedately so. And she wasn't unattractive—though he thought her more pretty than beautiful, and then in an average, unassuming sort of way. Since she was alone, he figured she must be part of the Mabry's or a guest's staff herself. Maybe some sort of aide who'd arrived early to make sure things were in order. There was a definite air of professionalism about her. Or, maybe it was breeding. Whoever and whatever she was, it was as clear as her reluctance to move that she was not a country girl. A country girl would have the sense to get in the truck before it started to rain and soaked her good jacket.

Or so he was thinking when he stopped in front of her.

"Do you work for the Mabrys?" she asked, her expression cautious.

"I'm a neighbor."

In his hurry to get back to his own emergency, which had struck before he'd responded to the Bauers' crisis, his only interest had been in hustling this woman into the truck so he could get back to his ranch. That was all that interested him now as his glance fell to her full, unadorned mouth.

He felt a quick tightening low in his gut.

Overlooking the unexpected sensation, he took a step toward her. "I own the ranch next to their place."

The best way to get her moving seemed to be to nudge her along himself. "Dave is in the hospital. He had a heart attack last night," he told her, more bluntly than he might have had she allowed him to ease into the news. Taking her by the elbow, he steered her toward the passenger door. "Jenny called me when she remembered she had a guest coming and asked me to meet your plane.

"Now, if you don't mind," he continued, doing his best to ignore the feel of her slender arm beneath soft wool, "we really do need to get going here."

With her now hurrying beside him, she darted a glance toward his chin. "Will he be all right?"

He had the truck's passenger door open when he finally looked at her. Even in boots with three-inch heels, the top of her head barely reached his shoulders. There were also little flecks of gold in her eyes. He noticed them as the concern in those pretty brown depths knitted the wood-brown wings of her eyebrows.

"It's too soon to tell."

"When will you know?"

Soft. Her unadorned mouth looked impossibly soft, he thought—and promptly jerked his glance from the appealing fullness of her lower lip.

His voice bore a faint edge. "Jenny said she'd call me later."

"Is the hospital nearby?"

"Can we have this conversation inside the truck?"

As frustrated as he already felt, the last thing he needed were reminders of how long it had been since he'd felt a woman's mouth—much less her body—moving beneath his own. He was a normal, red-blooded male, with a normal, red-blooded male's needs. The fact that those needs had been sorely neglected in the past couple of years wasn't anything he cared to consider. Especially because he had no intention of doing anything about them. Most especially because he wouldn't be doing anything about them with a city-type woman who wasn't the sort to attract him even if he had been looking for one.

Not sure why he was wasting time on such thoughts, frustrated with that, too, he started to help her inside.

Before he could, she'd murmured, "Of course," as if she couldn't imagine why he'd think otherwise—and climbed into the cab with far more grace than most women could have managed, considering the height of the running board and her heels.

He only had to deliver her to her destination. Reminding himself of that, he took off his well-worn Stetson so it wouldn't bump on the interior roof and climbed in on the other side. With his hat covering the small box on the seat between them, he started the engine.

"They air-evaced him to Missoula," he continued, picking up where he'd left off. "That's where Jenny called from."

She seemed fascinated by his hat. "Is that far?" she asked, looking up at the hat-dent in his dark hair.

"About two hundred and fifty miles."

He didn't mention how concerned he was about the older guy, or how he now needed to figure out what to do with his daughter. Jenny had watched his shy little Hanna for him since his housekeeper had quit a couple weeks ago. Right now, Hanna was with Kate Swenson, his ranch foreman's wife and part-time-cook-and-den-mother to the dozen hands it took to keep up his spread this time of year. Today, though, he needed Kate to run lunch out to his men before she left for her part-time job at the feed store that afternoon. It was spring roundup for branding and every hand was out bringing the calves and their mamas closer in. May weather was always a crapshoot and he had heifers with late dropping calves out there. The rain that had let up that morning could return as sleet by afternoon.

The woman beside him shifted in her seat and politely folded her hands in her lap. Her scent drifted toward him, something fresh, light, and like the woman herself, unexpectedly arousing.

With the staunch determination of a man accustomed to denying what distracted him, he kept his focus straight ahead.

Feeling totally out of her element, Sophie watched the rancher's jaw jerk and quickly looked away from the strong lines of his profile.

She wasn't at all certain what to think of the darkly handsome man providing her escort. He was far more…rugged, she supposed, and certainly less forthcoming than the refined sort of men she'd been exposed to most of her life. She knew men with power. Some had been born to it. Others had earned it working their way through the ranks of government, business or the military. Yet, not one of them had prepared her for—or possessed—the raw sort of masculinity this man exuded. Even his voice, its deep tones as rich and seductive as the finest brandy, disturbed her.

Tension radiated from his big body like heat. Intent on ignoring the odd way her own body seemed to absorb that tension, she focused on breathing out the quick anxiety she'd felt when she'd first seen him.

It had been deemed best by those who'd made her arrangements that the royal guard who'd accompanied her from Valdovia return there as soon as she'd been delivered to her aunt and uncle's home north of San Francisco. Since she was neither particularly glamorous, nor overly—or consistently—outrageous in her public behavior, she'd never been of interest to the U.S. media and its public. Only the Bauers, whom her aunt and uncle apparently trusted implicitly, knew of her royal family ties. Because of that it had been agreed there was no need for a bodyguard in this remote and sparsely populated place. According to her aunt, a guard would only call attention to her presence, anyway. Since she was to remain on the property, she'd been told that the Bauers would help her with whatever she needed.

Now fairly certain she wasn't being kidnapped for ransom or some sort of political statement—always a possibility among the rich and the royal, even those of little significance—her concern moved straight to the man whose health was in jeopardy.

"Will Mr. Bauer be all right?"

From his immediate response, it seemed her escort's thoughts were occupied with the man, too.

"Jenny said things could go either way."

"Do they have children?"

"A couple of grown daughters."

"Do they live here?"

His focus remained on the two-lane road that ran as straight as a stick for what appeared to be forever. The steady hum of the engine melded with the drone of the heater.

"They're up north."

North could have meant Canada for all she knew. She waited a few heartbeats, thinking he might offer something more about the couple her aunt had described as salt of the earth.

Nothing was forthcoming.

"I've obviously arrived at a stressful time," she said, figuring it futile to pry further, yet unable to simply let the matter go. "Is there anything I can do to help?"

The unexpected offer finally pulled Carter's glance toward her. He could think of any number of things an extra pair of hands could do. Hers, however, looked far too soft and manicured to be of any use to him. Then, there was her size. From what he'd felt of her slender biceps, she barely had enough muscle to pitch loose hay, much less move bales. The subtle air of refinement about her also seemed a pretty good indication that whatever culinary skills she might possess didn't lean toward brewing up gallons of coffee and pots of stew for ravenous ranch hands. There might be potential as a nanny there, but even if he discounted the reserve that struck him as more formal than he'd want a nanny to be, he wasn't about to turn his little girl's care over to a stranger.

Not even one with cautious but undeniably kind eyes and what sounded like genuine concern in her intriguing voice.

Not that she'd asked if she could help *him*, he reminded himself. She'd asked about helping the Bauers.

"I don't know what there is for you to do…unless you want to muck stalls and feed their horses." Since he regarded the possibility of her possessing the abilities—or the interest— to do either, right up there with the possibility of pigs flying, he continued even as she started to speak.

"Jenny asked me to take you to the hotel her sister manages in Eagle Prairie. That's about twenty miles up the road." The coffeehouse and cowboy bar-town wasn't much on the upscale amenities he figured a woman as polished as herself would be accustomed to. A few boutiques and restaurants had cropped up to cater to the wealthy buying up land to build their own private havens, but he'd never set foot in any of them. The only places he frequented with any regularity were the feed store, the post office and, when his hair started growing over his collar as it was now, the barber shop.

"I'll take you there right after we stop at the ranch. I have a problem with a calf." The antibiotic he'd just picked up from his vet wasn't doing the animal any good sitting in its vial. "The sooner I get it medicated, the better off it'll be."

At his mention of her uncle's horses, Sophie had been fully prepared to tell him she could, indeed, help with them. If there was anything she knew, it was horses. How to handle them, anyway. She'd never mucked a stall in her life. The change in her destination, however, had taken priority.

She started to tell him she hoped his calf would be all right. She focused instead on trying not to sound as alarmed by that change as she felt. "Why are you taking me to a hotel rather than the Mabrys' lodge?"

"Because there's no one at the lodge."

"But that's not what was arranged. There must be someone at the Mabrys. Who takes care of the horses?"

"Dave did," he replied flatly. "Jenny said his heart seized on him while he was hauling oats. I'll send over a hand to see they're watered and fed," he muttered, more to himself than to her, "or stable them at my place."

Aside from temporarily escaping the scrutiny of life in a royal fishbowl, the horses were one of the reasons Sophie had rather guiltily looked forward to her exile. She loved being with the big animals. She loved to ride. "Who decided I should go to this hotel?" she asked as those possibilities slipped from her.

The frown shadowing his carved features entered his voice. "Jenny did. She didn't think the Mabrys would want you to be there alone. Or that you would want to be out there alone yourself. It's a big place."

With all that Jenny Bauer had on her mind, it was as obvious as this man's defense of his neighbor that he thought she should be grateful for the woman's consideration. Sophie *was* grateful for it. Mrs. Bauer had far weightier matters to deal with than making arrangements for her care and feeding. Sophie just didn't want to have to show her identification when she checked into a room. The only ID she had with her was her passport and her Valdovian driver's license. The moment she produced the license it would be apparent she wasn't a US citizen. She'd then have to show her passport—

which contained seals identifying her as a member of the royal family and allowing her diplomatic immunity should the need for it arise.

It was her duty not to call attention to herself in any way. The entire point of her being there was to keep her hidden. She would not be hidden in a town. Especially one she suspected from what her aunt had told her was small enough that anyone who didn't live in the area would be noticed and talked about.

The last thing she wanted was for her name to leak out and for some intrepid reporter to conjure up headlines about her having been banished. Official word had it that she was on a scheduled holiday at an undisclosed location in the Alps. Skiing. Presumably, reporters and paparazzi were now freezing their way from Alta Badia to Zermatt attempting to capitalize on her most recent lapse of judgment.

Needing more information, she started to ask how she could contact Mrs. Bauer to ask exactly what arrangements had been made when a radio under the dashboard beeped.

Before she could say a word, the disapproving man beside her snatched up the handset with a succinct, "Carter. Over."

Looking relieved for the interruption, his attention shifted completely from her to his call—which left her free to wrestle with the constraints of not being able to explain anything about her situation to the compelling man who didn't impress her as being at all interested in hearing about it anyway.

Chapter Two

Years of practice allowed Sophie to present a reasonable facsimile of calm even when she felt totally unsettled inside. She would never master the cool serenity of Her Majesty, her mother or her older sisters. She'd always felt too restless for that. She had, however, learned to mask anxiety with composure. For the most part. After all, as she'd been reminded all her life, what she did, what she said and how she did and said it reflected directly on the crown.

Feeling that pressure now, she clasped her hands more tightly in her lap. The potential for a problem definitely existed with the change in her arrangements, but as long as Carter McLeod hadn't yet dropped her off at the hotel, she still had time to figure out what best to do.

It was just impossible to concentrate with him engaged in conversation beside her. Not that she understood what was being said, what with the heavy drawl in the male voice coming over the radio and the competing static crackle filling the truck's cab. As Carter spoke into the microphone he held in one big hand while he steered with the other, she couldn't understand half of what he said, either. She had no trouble comprehending authority when she heard it, though. He issued orders with the easy command of a general in her grandmother's guard.

"He shouldn't have had a quad down there. He's supposed to be riding bog. Have a wrangler take a string from the ramuda and meet him at the east fork. Ace can tow the quad back later with the hauler. Over.

"Don't worry about it now," he replied to the crackle and drawl that ended with the same indication to proceed. "Just get those strays out of there."

Something had broken down. Something else was where it shouldn't be. That was about all she could figure out before she heard him tell his caller that he was ten minutes away from wherever it was they were going, and that he'd call "Ace" to take care of whatever a quad was. Over and out.

A muscle in his jaw worked as he flicked a button on the handset and reached to turn a knob that changed the digital numbers on the channel display. "I have to take care of something," he muttered, more in explanation than apology, and was on to his next call before she could do much more than wonder what she'd so inadvertently gotten herself into.

She'd known she was coming to a foreign and unfamiliar place. It just hadn't occurred to her that the first person she'd meet would make her so aware of how alien she was here herself.

He'd said he owned a ranch. As he spoke, she heard him mention cows and calves. She'd visited genteel and manicured horse farms, but she'd never set foot on a cattle ranch in her life. She had no idea what running one involved. It seemed apparent, though, that he had his hands full with it at the moment.

He also had a sick animal to tend.

And he needed to deal with her.

Her last thought had her easing her arms over the disheartening sensation in her stomach. She was clearly a chore he didn't need.

The empty little pit inside her was far too familiar. She felt extraneous enough at times in her more customary surroundings. It did nothing for her already bruised ego to realize that she was now an imposition.

That discomfiting awareness had her looking everywhere but at her driver as the vast, ruggedly beautiful landscape rolled by her window. His deep voice surrounded her, a hint of a western drawl shading his resonant tones. There was none of the languid twang that underscored the other man's speech, though. What she heard mostly was self-possession, certainty and the taut, edgy control of a man accustomed to burying frustration.

That edge was what had her tightening her arms over the little void as they came upon a large, wrought-iron arch to the right of the road. That wide marker stood in what looked to her to be nothing but more vast, rolling and endless prairie. Or so it appeared before they passed beneath the iron letters that spelled *Mother Lode Ranch, est. 1886*. The road curved downward. Near the bottom of that incline, an oasis of trees appeared in the distance.

With Carter on his third call, they followed the narrow, graveled road toward a windbreak of poplar and cottonwood. Raw land soon gave way to a lawn desperately in need of mowing, a sprawling half-timbered house with a wrap-around log-pole porch and what would have been lovely flower beds had anyone bothered to weed them.

"Can't do it now. I have an errand to run first," she heard him say, apparently referring to his need to deliver her to the hotel. "I'll be there by noon."

They continued along the road as it curved behind the trees. Ahead of them stretched an imposing compound of barns and garages, outbuildings, stables and pens. Many of the structures were metal. Some, looking far older, were of the same log construction as the house. She barely noticed them. She was too busy trying not to dwell on having been reduced to an errand when he clicked the handset into place and pulled the truck to a stop.

Twenty feet ahead loomed a huge white barn, its wide doors open, its interior, from what she could see of it, cavernous. A complex of trailers and buildings formed an L a city block away.

The closest of those utilitarian structures was a long, log cabin with a short porch and two steps. In front of it, a woman in denim, a mauve thermal jacket and a cowboy hat loaded a large box into the bed of a mud-splattered, blue pickup truck. Her silver-gray braid swayed against her back as she shoved the box in, then started toward them.

Built like a fire plug, arms pumping, she bore down on the truck with a glance at her watch and purpose in her every step.

Killing the engine, Carter grabbed his hat and the small white box from the seat. "This won't take long," he muttered. "Give me five minutes and I'll get you where you need to go."

He could take all the time he needed, Sophie thought. She might have told him that, too, since she was in absolutely no hurry to go where he wanted to take her. But she'd barely murmured, "Certainly," before he'd opened the vehicle's door and stepped out.

Cold air rushed in. Along with it came an odd, distant bawling and the rushed tones of the woman's higher voice.

"It's good you're back," Carter heard Kate call as, slapping his hat on his head, he watched her over the open driver's door. "I only have fifty minutes to make the hour's drive out to Bald Knob to feed the boys. Ty wants you to meet him," she continued, only to forget to say where as her attention snagged on the woman in his truck.

Her voice dropped. "Is that her?"

At fifty, and being married for over half those years to a tobacco-chewing, ex-bronc buster with edges rough enough to sand wood, Carter figured Kate had earned every one of the wrinkles crinkling the corners of her keen hazel eyes. It was that unmistakable interest in her pleasantly rounded face that prompted his mental sigh. Her chatty outspoken curiosity about any stranger was exceeded only by her distrust of them and her persistence in getting answers, which meant he wouldn't get anything out of her about where to meet his foreman until her curiosity was satisfied. Kate knew about the Bauers' situation. She also knew he'd gone to pick up the woman they'd been expecting.

With Kate now behind him, ducking her head to see inside the cab of his truck, he started to introduce her to his passenger. That was when he realized he didn't know the woman's name. He hadn't wanted to know it. He'd just wanted her gone.

Ducking himself, he looked to the woman looking politely back at them. "This is Kate. Kate Swenson," he said, figuring he could start there. "She's my foreman's wife."

"And his men's cook," Kate offered, carefully scrutinizing the infinitely softer-looking woman across the seat.

From where he now stood in front of the open door, he watched the Mabrys' guest lean across the seat. Even in that awkward position, a certain elegance accompanied her motions as she offered her hand. "It's a pleasure to meet you,

Mrs. Swenson. I'm Sophie. Saxe…" she added, as if her surname were mere afterthought.

The older woman's curiosity compounded itself as she took her hand, gave it a sturdy shake. "You from England?"

The wing of one softly arched eyebrow sketched up. "England?"

"Your accent," Kate pointed out, blunt as ever. "Just wondered if you're from there."

"Oh. That." The quiet elegance remained as she gave a little shrug. "I didn't realize it was so noticeable. I'm not from there," she said, with a soft smile. "But I did go to school in London. For years, actually."

Kate had more questions. Carter could practically see them brewing beneath her dun leather hat when she backed up. She was in a hurry herself, though. Had she not been, as sure as sunrise she'd have stuck around to get them answered. Instead, looking truly torn, she excused herself, told him Ty would meet him where the men would corral a herd at Cougar Springs tomorrow and started for her truck.

"Where's Hanna?" he called after her, closing the door on the woman taking up time he didn't have to spare.

"In the cookhouse," Kate called back, still walking. "I'll send her to you in the barn."

"Keep her with you, will you? Give me five minutes and I'll come get her."

"I don't have five minutes, Carter. I'm sorry, but you need to take her with you now."

Frustration coiled like a snake in his gut. He couldn't be annoyed with Kate. She was already doing him a favor being late for her afternoon job by running the meals so far out to his men. The three busiest times of the year on a ranch were calving season and spring and fall roundup. Calving had started in February, so it was time now to round up the cows with their calves from the winter pastures. With nearly a thousand cow-calf pairs spread out over fifty square miles of land that ranged from bucolic to rugged, everyone in his hire was being pulled in two directions at once right now.

Reining in impatience, he tried not to sound as irritated, or maybe it was as discouraged, as he felt. "You know Hanna doesn't like being around big animals," he reminded her. "I don't have time to deal with her getting scared." He hated it when his little girl cried. He didn't want her to be afraid. Mostly, he didn't want to feel as powerless as he did whenever he was faced with her fears. "Just keep an eye on her a little longer, will you? There's no one else to do it right now."

From where Sophie sat, she watched the starch leave the older woman's spine. She was no more certain what to make of Kate Swenson than she was of the conversation taking place between the woman and her boss. She didn't look or dress like any cook Sophie had ever met. Between the curl-brimmed hat she wore over her waist-length gray braid, her boots and work clothes, she seemed more suited for work in the big barn than in a kitchen. She also appeared as no-nonsense as she'd sounded.

Something like pity seemed to enter her expression, though. Her exchange with Carter had been muffled by the truck's closed doors and windows, but Sophie had heard nearly every word.

"Five minutes, then," Kate called back, reluctance heavy in her tone. "But that's all. Your little girl's been waiting on you all morning, and hungry men get cranky when they have to wait to be fed."

His little girl? The tall, dark and disturbing rancher had a child?

Sophie didn't know what Carter said. Or if he said anything at all. Apparently interested only in having solved his immediate dilemma, he turned before the woman could change her mind. Within seconds, his powerful strides had carried him through the yawning mouth of the barn.

The woman temporarily tending his daughter headed back to the truck she'd been loading. From the low, covered porch of the rustic building just beyond it, she picked up a large insulated container. She'd just hefted it into the bed of the truck when the building's screen door opened.

A little wisp of a girl no more than four or five years old emerged to stand by a porch post near the steps. Her puffy pink jacket nearly swallowed her whole. Hugging a book to her chest, she lifted one hand to push back strands of hair that had escaped the pale blond ponytail listing at the top of her head.

Sophie couldn't tell if the girl's hair was uncombed or merely windblown. She couldn't hear what Kate said to her, either, but the child she assumed to be Hanna gave a small nod before the sturdy-looking woman shot an exasperated glance toward the barn and removed the last of the containers from the porch.

Sophie's attention fastened on the child. The little girl remained motionless by the post. From her diffidence, it almost seemed as if she sensed she was in the way, somehow. Or, with the cook's clear impatience to leave, perhaps that she knew her care was regarded by some as an unavoidable duty.

Hating the thought, Sophie climbed down from the truck's cab. Gravel crunched beneath her boots, undoubtedly ruining their heels. But the possibility that the child might be feeling as lost as she looked was all she considered just then.

Kate stopped what she was doing at her approach. The shy-looking little girl warily backed toward the building's door.

Sophie offered them both a smile, though that easy expression faltered slightly as the older woman gave her neat slacks and jacket a decidedly thorough once-over.

"Something I can do for you?" Kate asked, working her way back up to the tasteful pearl studs in Sophie's ears.

Sophie wasn't accustomed to such blunt assessments. In public, especially, she knew that what she wore and how she held herself was subject to inspection and critique. But in her country, people seemed more polite about their scrutiny. To her face, anyway. Carter's appraisal had been even more thorough than Kate's. More…invasive, she supposed, though she couldn't put her finger on what else about it had so unnerved her. Unless it was because his interest had seemed more in what lay beneath the tailored wool than how it was cut and styled—before that interest had been summarily dismissed.

"I wondered if I could help," Sophie explained, forcing her thoughts back to the man's child. "If you can't leave because the little girl needs tending, she's welcome to wait with me in the truck. I'm not doing anything but waiting for Mr. McLeod."

Dismissal of another sort came with the shake of the woman's head. "That's kind of you, miss. But we don't impose on strangers."

"You wouldn't be imposing. Truly," Sophie hurried to assure her. "It's not as if I have anywhere else to go," she explained, thinking the woman had no idea how true that was. "And I'm not a total stranger. I know the Mabrys." Where she came from, connections could be nearly as important as blood. "Since they have land not far from here, you know them, too. Don't you?"

"I only know of them," Kate dismissed, then hesitated. "I know Carter thinks highly of the mister," she admitted. "He wouldn't run their cattle with his own if he didn't. And the Bauers feel kindly toward them, what with all the charity work they do."

Considering, Kate glanced at her watch, eyed her once more.

"He does tend to lose track of time when he's tending an animal." The admission prompted the quick thinning of her mouth. "Maybe leaving her with you isn't a bad idea," she conceded, succumbing to practicality. "His idea of five minutes can sometimes be half an hour, and I'm running later here by the second."

Turning her back to Hanna, she lowered her voice. "She's a good child. Quiet little thing. She won't give you any problem while you're waiting."

Sophie didn't mind the wait. The longer the child's father took, the longer she avoided going into town. Still, considering what the woman had just said about Carter losing track of time, she did wonder for his daughter's sake just how long little Hanna might have to wait with her.

"Will her mother be here soon?"

The soft spot the cook had for the child apparently didn't extend to the woman who'd given her birth. The quick chill in her expression entered her still-quiet voice.

"That woman hasn't set foot in these parts since she took Hanna and walked out a couple years ago," she muttered, half under her breath. "The only one coming for Hanna will be Carter."

Confused, Sophie looked to where Hanna stood hugging her book.

"Her mother decided she didn't want her," Kate explained, since the child was obviously there now. "She sent some friend to leave her with Carter a few months back.

"Hanna?" she called, her tone returning to normal as she

motioned the little girl over. "Come meet Miss Sophie. I have to go, so you can sit with her while you wait for your daddy."

Though Hanna looked a little uncertain, she dutifully descended the two weathered steps leading from the porch. Watching her, Sophie had to admit she hadn't considered that her rugged and reluctant escort might have offspring. She hadn't considered that he would have a wife for that matter. Or have had one, anyway. He'd seemed too distant, too self-contained to be vulnerable to any woman.

Had she known he had a child, though, she would have assumed he had a son. She would not have imagined him having the delicate, sweet-faced angel shyly waiting for Sophie to speak to her.

Feeling her heart squeeze at that painful reticence, Sophie held out her hand and quietly asked Hanna if she wanted to sit in the truck. The child's only response was a nod, and to hug her book a little tighter.

Having handed off her temporary charge, Kate closed the tailgate of the truck with a solid clang.

At that clear indication that the woman would now be departing, Sophie dropped her hand. Not wanting the child to be frightened of her, she offered another smile and asked Hanna if she wanted to lead the way to her father's truck. Seeming to think taking the lead was okay, she marched across the compound to the big silver vehicle, her high ponytail bobbing, and climbed in on her own when Sophie opened the door for her.

Once inside, she scooted as far over to the driver's side as she could get. By the time Sophie settled herself on the charcoal-colored fabric of the bench seat, the little girl was hugging her book once more.

Her sober eyes were as gray as her father's. Her hair,

though, pale blond and definitely uncombed, made Sophie wonder if the rest of her fair coloring came from her mother.

Knowing that the child's mother didn't want her, tugged at every maternal instinct Sophie possessed. As protected as she had been as a child, as she still was in ways she could gladly live without, she couldn't imagine how that sort of maternal abandonment must feel.

The knowledge that the woman had first left the little girl's father made her wonder if Carter had felt abandoned, too. And betrayed, angry, hurt and all the other disappointments that came with putting faith in the wrong person. If, maybe, he lived with that discouraging sense of disillusionment even now.

The thought disturbed her. She was all too familiar with betrayal, and with the self-doubt and recriminations that came with having put trust in the wrong people. Men in particular. She knew nothing about this particular man, though, other than that he was apparently there for his neighbors and his animals when they needed him. Still, she strongly suspected he hadn't been at all prepared to have his daughter suddenly dropped on his doorstep.

She ducked her head, tried to read the jacket of the book Hanna held upside down and snug against her quilted, pink jacket. An embroidered lavender butterfly danced on one cuff. The shoelaces of her little pink sneakers were lavender, too.

"Is that book one of your favorites?" she asked, hoping to put the too-quiet child at ease.

Her nod was so slight her ponytail barely moved.

"Can you tell me what it's about?"

"A ballerina," came her quiet voice.

"A ballerina? May I see?

"I studied ballet for years," she confided as Hanna cautiously held out her book. "I didn't much care for the barre work…that's this," she said, indicating an image of a young girl in a tutu, one hand on the waist-high barre attached to a huge mirror. The exercises had simply been more regimentation in a life already filled with rules and protocols. "But I loved pirouettes. And runs and leaps," she confided. "Those were my favorites."

She turned a page, looked back to the pretty eyes that now seemed more intrigued than cautious.

Sophie tipped the page toward her. "Can you hold your arms like that?"

Hanna shook her head, murmured, "No."

"Do you want to learn how?"

"Can I?"

Sophie grinned. "Absolutely."

If the clouds had allowed him to check the position of the sun, Carter would have looked up to estimate the time as he left the barn. With the sky still solid gray, he checked his watch, instead.

Swearing, he started across the compound to get his daughter. He'd told Kate he'd be five minutes. He'd been twenty. As soon as he had Hanna, Kate could leave and he'd see who he could raise on the CB to watch his little girl for him while he ran the woman he'd all but forgotten about into town.

Kate's truck was gone.

His glance cut from the space the vehicle had occupied to the cookhouse no one would use until supper that evening.

He knew Kate wouldn't have taken Hanna with her. He just wasn't sure what she'd done with her until his search swept past his own truck and caught on the people inside.

Hanna sat in the middle of the seat, on her knees, judging

from her height. She had her arms stretched up and curved over her head. The dark-haired woman he'd left waiting for him seemed to be positioning Hanna's fingers with her own.

The Mabrys' guest sat angled with her back to him. Crossing in front of the truck, he caught her profile—and her encouraging smile—as he rounded the fender.

His little girl looked totally enthralled.

Both females seemed perfectly oblivious to him until he opened the driver's door. The moment he did, Hanna's arms fell. Sophie's smile evaporated like water on a hot skillet.

His scowl for his cook's departure remained. He did, though, consciously gentle his voice for his little girl.

"Where's Kate?" he asked her.

Hanna's narrow shoulders lifted to her ears. "She left."

From behind where Hanna still knelt on the bench seat, the woman with her leaned forward.

"I offered to keep Hanna with me," Sophie explained, feeling compelled to come to Kate's defense. Especially with him looking so fierce. "There didn't seem to be any point in her waiting while I was sitting here doing nothing. Hanna and I had a nice time."

The smile that had died at the sight of him returned for his daughter. "Didn't we?" she asked her.

Hanna returned to being subdued. Giving Sophie a nod, she sank to her little backside and straightened out her legs.

Sliding in next to his daughter, Carter settled behind the wheel. His wide shoulders seemed to take up half the seat. The sheer force of his presence seemed to fill the rest of the cab. Or, maybe, it was the way his quicksilver eyes caught hers that seemed to rob the oxygen from the remaining space.

His glance slid to her mouth. As if catching himself, he deliberately jerked his attention to starting the truck.

"Thanks for watching her." He'd left the keys in the ignition. With the quick twist of his wrist, the low hum of the engine joined the preoccupied tone of his voice. "It's been a busy morning.

"Jenny can't come get you today," he then said to Hanna. His palm settled on her short legs, his big, masculine hand looking huge and decidedly incongruous against the feminine pink denim. "I'll call Truly to see if you can stay with her. You remember meeting Truly, don't you?" he asked, giving her knees a reassuring pat before putting the vehicle into gear. "Doc Scott's wife?"

"She has big boys."

"They're big," he agreed. "But they're not much older than you." Seeming to have missed her concern, he moved on to Plan B. "If Truly isn't available," he continued, the truck bouncing a little as they headed up the road they'd come down, "we'll try Kate's daughter-in-law. You can come with me, first, though. We need to get Miss Saxe to town."

Saxe.

Sophie had given the name because it was easy. And it was hers. Part of it anyway. The entire royal family used the hyphenated version in situations where a full, legal surname was necessary. The pared down version suited her purposes here, however, even though she strongly suspected that no one other than a student of history, or a rabid royal watcher, would recognize her country's royal house. England had its Royal House of Windsor. Monaco, its princely Grimaldi. While Valdovia might be known in the States, the Royal House of Saxe-Savoyard probably was not.

Still, Sophie Saxe was far more likely to fly under the radar than Sophia Victoria Mathilde Saxe-Savoyard.

And that was the name on her passport.

The man whose work-roughened hand had protectively settled once more on pink denim was about to take her where she truly didn't want to go. Where she couldn't go without calling attention to herself just by opening her mouth.

For her family's and her country's sake, she was desperate to not mess up her exile. Being honest with herself, she didn't want to mess it up for her own sake. She knew from experience that it took forever to get back into the good graces of her grandmother, and those of the royal secretary who arranged her own schedule. She'd be lost if she was denied the few worthwhile duties she did perform.

Then, there was this man's daughter's obvious reluctance to spend the day with bigger, probably teasing and more energetic boys.

They'd almost reached the sprawling log house with the wraparound porch. In another few moments, they'd be past it.

"Mr. McLeod. Wait. Please," she asked, doing her best to mask her desperation. "You don't need to waste your time taking me into town now. It's obvious you have a lot to do today," she pointed out, conscious of the way his eyebrows merged. "Since I don't know anyone in town and have no idea what I'll do there, anyway, why don't I stay with Hanna myself? That will save you the need to find someone else now, and you won't need to take me into town until your work for the day is finished."

That would at least give her time to call her Aunt Bree and ask her to send the plane back for her. If that couldn't be arranged by evening and she had to spend the night, her aunt could put the room at the hotel in the Mabrys' name. Sophie was thinking the room could be put on their credit card, too, when Hanna perked up and looked to her dad.

"Can she, daddy? Please? I'll be good for her," she insisted, swiping back a stray hair as she nodded. "I promise. She's a ballerina."

Carter had no idea what threw him the most just then; the promise and the plea that hit him far harder than he wanted to admit. Or his daughter's unanticipated, totally unexpected revelation about his passenger.

The image of an impossibly graceful, willowy dancer with mile-long legs flashed in his mind. He'd never been to a ballet in his life. He had no desire to attend one, either. But with the subtle elegance in Sophie's simplest movements, he supposed she had the grace. As his glance skimmed the length of her tailored slacks, he figured she definitely had the legs.

"You're a ballerina?"

Sophie knew how to evade, versed in diplomacy as she'd been. What she couldn't do with any conviction whatsoever was lie.

"My parents thought ballet a necessary part of my education, so I did have about ten years of training. I was never part of a troupe, though," she admitted, sticking with the truth. Part of it, anyway. What she didn't care to share was that the training had been an effort to counter the unrefined, tomboy tendencies that had plagued her throughout her childhood. She'd have been far happier climbing a tree. Having broken her arm in a fall from one when she'd been seven years old had, however, ended that particular pleasure. "My only involvement with it now is as a volunteer at the academy where I studied."

"You teach?"

Teaching dance wouldn't have been dignified. Not according to Valdovia's royal protocol, anyway. Just as royals performing in public was frowned upon, it wouldn't have been appropriate for her to work wearing a leotard. "I'm involved more with fundraising." Her present position was honorary chairwoman of the Royal Academie de Ballet. She omitted that, too. Along with the fact that her position was mostly a token one, held as a representative of the royal family.

"But I do volunteer work with children," she hurried to explain, wanting him to know she wasn't without experience with the four-foot-and-under crowd. "I read to them at libraries and hospitals and do art projects with them in schools."

"You do charity work, then."

The flatness of his tone removed any question.

"You could call it that," she conceded. It hardly seemed charity, though, when she got back as much from the young ones as she gave. "I just think of it more as spending time with them."

His glance darted to her left hand. It was clasped in her right, her fingers covered. "Do you have kids of your own?"

"Not yet." Though she hoped to. Someday. "I need a husband first."

His ridiculously long-lashed eyes narrowed on hers. She had no idea what he was thinking as his glance moved over her face, slid slowly down to her knees. She knew only that, in her circles, a man she'd just barely met wouldn't be impudent enough to study her so boldly.

But this man had no idea who she was. He didn't know her as anyone other than a woman he'd picked up for his neighbors.

No one here knew her.

No one.

The incredible thought echoed in her head, an odd mantra that took a few rather long moments to sink in. When it finally did, the unbelievably free sensation that came with it made it feel as if a glass wall surrounding her had just shattered.

She also realized that he had her stomach feeling oddly jumpy—before it occurred to her that he'd stopped the truck.

"How do you know the Mabrys?"

She swallowed, torn between relishing her moment of freedom and being more rattled by his unapologetic masculinity than she was about to admit.

Her tone, however, remained commendably calm. "My parents have known them for years." Like her partial name, the response was true. As far as it went. "I don't remember ever not knowing them."

"So, you're family friends," Carter concluded.

"I certainly hope so."

He'd thought at first she might be some sort of an aide. Something about her, though, the way she held herself, maybe, hadn't quite fit that handy cubbyhole. Her family being old friends of the Mabrys made more sense to him. Especially given what she'd told him about herself. It also explained volumes about her.

What he knew about ballet could be etched on the tip of a nettle, but her involvement with it explained a little of the polish that spoke of a world the polar opposite of his own. A world of sophistication, culture, class. And, with her connection to the Mabrys, a world of privilege.

All that interested him at the moment, however, was her apparently considerable experience with kids—and his daughter's unusual and obvious comfort with her. In the five months since she'd been back home, this was the first time Hanna had shown anything other than marginal enthusiasm about anything.

Feeling protective in the extreme, he caught the plea still in his little Hanna's eyes.

Her promise to be good hit him all over again. She hadn't

given him a moment's trouble since her mother had sent her back. As quiet as she tended to be, there were times he hardly knew she was there.

Guilt jerked hard. He hated how little time he and everyone else had for her right now. He also couldn't deny the practicality of this woman's surprisingly accommodating suggestion. Being friends of Matt Mabry, it wasn't as if she didn't have references, either.

"Okay, then," he conceded, putting more weight on his daughter's ease with her than anything else. "If you're willing to stay, I'd appreciate the help." The need to deny the effect of her smile kicked in an instant before he put the truck into gear. "But just for today."

Chapter Three

"It'll be best if you both stay inside the house." Carter pulled open the glass storm door on the back porch, pushed the heavy inner door wide. "A greenhorn can find herself in trouble if she gets to poking around on her own, Miss Saxe. Hanna likes being inside rather than out, anyway."

Holding the doors, he waited for both females to enter the mud room that had changed little since his birth. His daughter walked in first, carrying her book as if it were something precious. The woman who'd so unexpectedly offered to help them out came in behind her, passing near enough for him to breathe the taunting scent of her perfume. Clean, fresh, yet undeniably sensual, the scent hit his lungs with the impact of a fist.

He let both doors bang shut behind him.

"Call me, Sophie. Please," she asked of his back as he strode past the washer, dryer, freezer and storage cabinets. A row of old boots lined the wall by the inner door. Above them, pegs held an old quilted parka and his heavy canvas duster.

As much from habit as manners, he pulled off his hat before he entered the house. Hanging it on an empty peg, he combed his hair back with his fingers and turned to see her watching him.

"What is a greenhorn?"

"It's a tenderfoot," he explained, when he'd closed the door behind her. "A rookie."

He didn't bother to take off his jacket. Figuring he wouldn't be inside all that long, he left it hanging open over his heavy chambray shirt. His scarred boots thudding on hardwood, he crossed to the granite-topped center island he wouldn't be able to finish re-staining until after fall roundup.

The woman in the tailored tweed remained by the back door with her hands clasped sedately in front of her. The quiet air of breeding about her seemed even more noticeable now that she'd entered his disordered domain. Not caring to consider what she thought of his half-finished, re-remodeling project, he focused on her confusion.

"It's someone who doesn't know their way around a ranch," he said, since she still looked puzzled by the terminology. Between the saws, blades and tools in the mechanic's garage, the big animals and equipment in the barns and stables, the bigger animals in the corrals and out on the range, the porcupines, snakes and skunks, he didn't want to even consider the potential problems she could run into wandering out there alone with his child. "You'll both be safe in the house."

She was hardly dressed for the outdoors, anyway.

"We'll stay inside then."

He appreciated her easy concession. Still, his frustration remained on simmer as defensiveness joined it. Breakfast dishes sat unwashed in the sink. The load of clothes he'd pulled from the dryer to find clean socks for Hanna spilled from the end of the long monastery table he'd rescued from the shed his ex-wife had stored it in. His great-grandfather had brought it up from a mission in Texas before Montana was even a state. He liked it far better than the black lacquer square she'd taken with her.

"Things aren't usually so chaotic around here," he muttered. Why he wanted her to know that, he wasn't quite sure. He did know that he didn't like feeling he had to apologize. Or, maybe, what he didn't like was that her polish made him feel the need to. "It's a busy time of year."

"You don't have domestic help?"

"My housekeeper quit a couple of weeks ago. To take care of her daughter's family over in Billings," he explained, so she wouldn't think he'd done something to run the woman off. "She was watching Hanna for me."

The need to hire someone soon grew more pressing every day. The ads he'd put on the bulletin board at the co-op in town and the local weekly newspaper had only netted him two responses, though. Both had been for part-time day help.

He needed full-time live-in.

He needed twelve more hours in every day so he could spend a few of them with his daughter.

He needed to stop wasting the time he had now.

He motioned to Hanna. "Come on, sweetheart." With a yank of the worn denim above his knees, he crouched down as she walked up to him. "Let's get you out of your jacket."

"Is Miss Sophie going to stay?"

"She is."

"Are you?"

His mouth thinned before he shook his head. "You know I can't do that, honey. I have work to do. I'll see you tonight, though." He smoothed back a strand of her untidy hair. Because Wiley, his barn boy, had called him a little before five about the calf, he hadn't had time to help her brush it. He'd pretty much dressed her in her sleep and carried her to the cookhouse for Kate to watch. "Okay?"

Hanna echoed him with a quiet, "'Kay."

Sophie heard disappointment in both of their voices. Feeling like an intruder as Carter gave his daughter a tight hug, she surreptitiously glanced around the spacious and surprising room. It was a bit cluttered with dishes, laundry and the papers that threatened to overtake the desk in the alcove by the antique-looking kitchen table, but what struck her most was the odd sterility about it. The only permanent items on the long, shining, black granite counters were a coffee pot and a toaster.

The worn planking on the floors and walls of the utility room had seemed as serviceable and timeworn as the split-log exterior of the house. This room had obviously undergone renovation. The surprisingly modern and sophisticated kitchen with its stainless-steel appliances and lacquer-and-glass cabinetry seemed to be in transition again, though. Half of the wood shined a deep Chinese red. The other half gleamed a warm pecan. From the sanding marks where much of the color on one side of the island had been removed it seemed the warmer wood tone would eventually prevail.

Wondering if his ex-wife had walked out in the midst of the work, and curious about whose taste—his or hers—had been overridden, her focus shifted to the man himself. The brawny cattleman exhibited extraordinary patience working down the stuck zipper on his child's jacket. Yet, every other trait he seemed to possess defied everything she'd heard about the West and ranchers and cowboys being laid-back. The muscles in his big body seemed taut as trip wires when he rose and headed for the desk in the alcove.

"Cell phone service is spotty to nonexistent in these parts." That tension seemed to radiate like sound waves as he looked back to motion her to him. "CB is how we communicate around here. Citizens' band," he explained, apparently sensing she'd been about to ask.

"This is only good if I'm in the truck, though," he continued, showing her which switches to flip, what channel to use. "We carry walkie-talkies on the range, but they don't reach this far. If there's an emergency and you can't get me in the truck, call Truly Scott on the landline. She's about five miles south of where I picked you up."

Grabbing a pen, he wrote a number on a small pad, underscored it with a bold, single slash. He left it propped next to the digital phone by a large and leaning stack of mail.

The sight of the telephone reminded her that she needed to use one.

"Do you mind if I make a call?" she asked, thinking of Dave and Jenny Bauer. Her personal dilemma had her stomach in a bit of a knot, but it was hardly life and death. The Bauers' situation truly could be.

"I should let the Mabrys know where I am. They'll want to know what's going on with the Bauers, too." Given the woman's priorities that morning, it was entirely possible Jenny hadn't yet called her aunt. "They may want to see if they can help. Or," she added, because she was closer and perfectly capable, "they can tell me what I can do for them."

There were other things he needed to tell her. Her easy

thoughtfulness for his neighbors overrode them for the moment, though. Considering how quickly she'd asked the first time what she could do to help, and how she'd offered to help him out with Hanna now, that kindness seemed to come to her as naturally as breathing.

She was near enough for him to notice the exquisitely soft look of her skin, and the disturbing scent of her undoubtedly expensive perfume. Conscious of the unwanted effects of her presence on his body, well-honed survival instincts kicked firmly into place.

"When you call, leave a message for Matt that I'll bring his horses over and stable them here." Horses were infinitely safer to think about. With a horse, a man learned what to expect. With a woman, he never did. "That way, he won't have to make arrangements for someone to take care of them. It's branding time," he told her, having no time now to explain the sort of dirty, noisy, back-breaking work that entailed—in case she was about to ask. "He'd be hard pressed to find a hand free to help him, anyway."

Feeling the need for a little distance, he turned around to look for his little girl.

She stood near the far end of the island, her brow lowered in concentration, her arms looped out in front of her. With her palms facing, it looked as if she was trying to touch her thumbs with their respective middle fingers.

"What are you doing?" he asked.

"Practicing," came her matter-of-fact reply.

"Her hand poses," Sophie clarified for him. "What she's doing is part of first position."

"Right," he muttered. "Look," he said, figuring she was now even with him for "greenhorn." "I've got to go. Is there anything you're going to need before I do?"

The soft wing of one eyebrow arched. "Would you have a kettle? And a tea pot?"

She might as well have asked for champagne and caviar. It wasn't that he'd never had the bubbly French wine or the briny fish eggs he'd thought more suited for bait. His ex had been obsessed with what she'd referred to as "civilized things." It was just that his personal tastes were far heartier. Or, more likely, just less refined. He preferred meat and potatoes. Beer and bourbon.

"Sorry." He definitely didn't do hot tea. "Don't have either. No tea for that matter. We're coffee drinkers around here." The stronger, the better.

"Then just my bags, please."

"I'll leave them in the mudroom," he told her. He'd planned to bring them in, anyway. He needed the room for equipment. "There's food in the fridge and a television in the den. Hanna can show you around."

With that, he dropped a kiss to the top of his little girl's head and grabbed his hat from its peg when he passed through the kitchen door.

His temporary sitter's designer luggage was sitting where he'd told her he'd put it when he turned the nose of the truck toward the rutted road leading to where his men were herding stock toward Bald Knob. Now that he had covered his bases on the home front—for the moment, anyway—nothing demanded his attention now but work. He would have been as insensitive as a rock not to be grateful for that. Not that sensitivity was his strong suit. Still, as much as he appreciated the unexpected help of the undeniably refined, tea-drinking member of the society set, he couldn't help but think the Fates truly twisted for dumping her in the middle of his fifty square miles of rugged rangeland, creeks, coyotes and cattle. He'd take what he could get, though. For now.

* * *

Sophie had dozed off. She just hadn't realized it until she became aware of sleep tingles in the leg folded beneath her.

Lifting her head from the back of the deep leather sofa, she glanced at the brass clock in the crowded, floor-to-ceiling bookcase. The last time she'd checked the hour it had been nearing nine o'clock. The hands indicated it was now after ten.

With one hand she rubbed her leg. With the other, she moved the catalogue she'd fallen asleep perusing from her lap to the sofa's wide, curved arm. She didn't know if she'd imagined the sound in her sleep or if it was what had wakened her, but she thought she'd heard the click of a closing door.

The anxiety she'd tried to avoid by keeping herself occupied was back.

She needed to stay here. Her Aunt Bree hadn't liked the idea of her being in town alone any better than Sophie had liked it herself. Since her grandmother's advisors wanted her out of sight, her Uncle Matt had insisted she would be just as hidden from potential discovery by the press and just as secure with Carter McLeod as she would have been at their lodge. According to him, Carter was a breed apart, a fair man of utter integrity. He'd asked her to have Carter call him when he returned from the range so he could ask Carter himself to watch out for her until arrangements to send other staff to the lodge could be made.

Because she had no other alternative, she hadn't told her uncle she thought his upstanding and principled friend barely tolerated her—and then, only because of his child.

The sofa sat in the middle of the room, facing the wall of bookcases and a flat screen television. Glancing over its back, she looked through the open double doors to the front entry that separated the nearly empty living and dining rooms. She heard nothing in the stillness of the house, though. Nothing beyond the quiet beat of the rain on the windows. Since Hanna's father would probably come in through the kitchen, she wasn't sure she would hear his return, anyway.

The sprawling home had living areas in the front and bedrooms along a side wing. From the soaring height of the living room and the newer looking wood floors in the front of the structure, she had the sense that the area had been added on in the past several years. The architecture with its high log beams seemed a more modern rendition of the other parts of the house, but what there was of the decor, specifically the stainless-steel-and-glass entry table and the glass-and-steel mantel on the stone fireplace, seemed an odd blend of urban and rustic.

She liked the room she sat in now better. Hanna had called it the "den." Sophie supposed it did feel like a place a person could hibernate in. To her, though, the decidedly masculine space seemed more a man's drawing room or library. Dark, polished wood wainscoting bisected the two walls not filled with equally beautiful bookcases and a gray stone fireplace. A large desk, its green blotter covered with what she'd realized were invoices and payroll records before she'd quickly changed the direction of her roaming, held a tobacco box and a rack of pipes. Both looked old and antique.

A framed photograph of Hanna, somewhere around two-years-old and holding the then not-so-bedraggled stuffed bunny she'd fallen asleep with, sat beside a photo of a shorter-haired and bespectacled version of Carter with his arm around a pretty redhead and two grinning boys. A relative, she assumed from the cleft in his chin, the strong jaw line and the sharp, noble nose. Perhaps, a brother.

Just as she hadn't considered him having had a wife or

child, she hadn't thought of him as having familial connections until she'd seen that photo. Despite the number of people he'd communicated with in her presence, there had been such an emotionally solitary air about him that he seemed a force completely unto himself.

"Sorry I'm so late."

Carter's deep voice came from behind her. Glancing around at the door again, her elbow hit the catalogue on the arm of the chair.

It landed with a soft plop on the rug.

He stood in the doorway, filling the space with his tall, impressive body, and pulling her apprehension front and center.

"No need to get up," he said, looking very large—and very tired—as he entered the room.

The stubble shadowing his jaw appeared considerably darker than she'd last seen it, but the hat dent in his dark hair had been marginally decreased on one side. Presumably because he'd run his fingers through it there.

A streak of dirt slashed one cheek. The dampness of his shirt cuffs indicated that he'd just washed his hands. The rest of him, however, looked as if he'd been wrestling something large and cantankerous in the mud.

She expected to see mud on his boots, too, when he rounded the sofa and bent to pick up what had fallen. The legs of his jeans were wet and dirty from knee to hem, but he'd taken off his boots—which, she figured, explained why she hadn't heard him moving in the hall.

Despite his insistence that she stay put, and embarrassed to be caught in her stocking feet, she self-consciously pulled on her own boots. The moment they were zipped, she smoothed the cuffs of her slacks over them and rose to move to the middle of the long sofa.

Claiming more space hadn't been necessary. As she'd risen, he'd tossed the catalogue onto the stack of flying and ranching magazines on the coffee table, and moved back himself. His attention wasn't on her. It was on the wood and kindling stacked in the niche by the dark fireplace.

"It's cold in here. Why didn't you build a fire?"

"Because I didn't know how," she said with a shrug.

It had occurred to Sophie several hours earlier that she should have paid more attention to the servants when they'd laid and stoked fires at the palace. Her only thought now was that he didn't look terribly amenable to the conversation she needed to have with him.

"I would have tried to build one," she admitted, because she had considered it. "But I knew you had reservations about leaving me here with your daughter. Since you already have so many worries, I thought it best not to add to them by filling your house with smoke."

Carter hadn't slowed down since his feet had hit the carpet long before sunup that morning. As late as it was now, sore and tired from wrestling calves and pretty sure he smelled like one, all he wanted was a hot shower and a bed. What he did not want was to be so aware of the kindness in the small, guarded smile she gave him. Or the quiet sort of understanding that would have made him even more uncomfortable if he'd had the energy to consider her acknowledgment of his concerns. With fatigue clawing at his bones, he was simply too tired to deny the appeal of her soft expression and the sympathy in her voice.

"I hope I didn't presume too much," Sophie continued, thinking he didn't appear quite as unapproachable as she'd first thought. "But I told Hanna you'd come say good-night when you returned. After that...if you wouldn't mind," she qualified, since she was hardly in a position to order him around, "Matthew would like you to call him."

Carter shoved his fingers through his hair, let his hands fall to jam on his hips. He felt fairly certain Matt wanted to make sure taking care of his horses wouldn't be too much trouble. He knew what a busy time of year it was. "I'll call him in the morning." Seeing nothing urgent there, he relegated the call to his to-do list for tomorrow. "And I was just in with Hanna."

His little girl was safely in her bed, sound asleep and smelling of soap and toothpaste. Seeing her so peaceful and well tended had filled him with as much guilt as relief. The relief he'd momentarily indulged. The guilt he simply added to the well of it buried beneath the need to focus on whatever situation demanded his attention at the moment. "But I didn't want to wake her up."

Like he'd obviously wakened her caretaker, he thought, wondering at the consternation shadowing her features. "How was she today?"

A small sleep crease from the sofa or one of its pillows marred his temporary sitter's otherwise smooth cheek. Even if it hadn't been such a long day, presumably for her, too, since she'd been traveling, the catalogue of tack she'd looked to for entertainment surely would have put her to sleep. He couldn't imagine anything more boring for her than reading descriptions of lassos and cinches or trying to figure out what the leather and metal contraptions were for.

"She had a good day. Busy," she qualified, the odd dismay he'd seen in her giving way to something less concerning. "But good, I think."

Her long, rather plain brown hair remained tightly restrained, smoothed back as it was from her face. Yet, the small smile that emerged as she spoke of his daughter made her features seem more delicate than he'd recalled from that morning. Softer, somehow.

He missed that about a woman; that softness.

"We spent most of the morning reading and drawing, and the afternoon and evening with puzzles and watching movies," she told him, distracting him from the unwanted admission. "Actually, one movie. Twice. *Cinderella* seems to be her favorite."

"I thought it was *Beauty and the Beast*."

"Girls are known to change their minds." At his frown, she gave a philosophical shrug. "I imagine between now and when she grows up, she'll change her mind about a lot of things."

He seemed to find no encouragement at all in the friendly warning. In the space of seconds, cynicism shadowed the carved lines of his face, entered the deep tones of his voice.

"I'm familiar with the female ability to swear she likes one thing," he assured her, "only to decide she wants something else. I really hope Hanna hasn't inherited that particular gene."

The disquiet Sophie felt the moment he'd dismissed calling her uncle tonight merged with a different sort of concern. It was as apparent as the lines of fatigue carved in Carter's face, that he wasn't referring to something as inconsequential as his daughter's choice of fairy tale. The first hour Sophie had spent with his little girl had made her painfully aware of how needy Hanna was—and of how fearful she seemed to be of letting her need for attention show. Hanna had almost seemed to brace her little self for rejection as she'd tentatively shown Sophie the first of her favorite possessions. It had been as if she expected to be shooed away or that she had somehow been made to feel that what she wanted to share was unimportant, or an imposition.

There'd also been the worry that had looked far too old for such innocent little eyes when Hanna had looked out the back window and asked if her daddy would come home.

Not come home soon.

Come home. Period.

"I'm sorry." Sophie spoke the words quietly. "For Hanna," she told him, because the child couldn't articulate the hurts and fears that made her feel so insecure. "And for you.

"Kate told me your wife left with Hanna," she explained as his brow slammed low, "and that she sent her back to you a few months ago. I can only imagine how difficult her changes of heart have been for both of you."

While the child remained too naive to mask her emotions, the man who had sired her possessed infinitely thicker armor. The bitterness in his tone had totally betrayed the resentment he felt toward his wife. Yet, in the time it took for him to cross his arms over his broad chest and narrow his eyes on hers, he'd masked whatever else his fatigue might have allowed him to betray.

For a moment, Carter said nothing. There wasn't much that caught him off guard anymore, but this woman had. Both with her sympathy and with her reason for it.

What his busybody cook had shared didn't particularly bother him. Half the county knew of his divorce, partly because there weren't that many people in it. Mostly because those there were knew, or knew of, nearly everyone else. Among the permanent residents, anyway. Anyone of a mind to keep track of the gossip also knew that a year and a half after she'd left, Tiffany had sent Hanna back to him straight out of the blue, along with all her clothes and toys.

He supposed he could see how the woman watching him now might care about the effects of Tiffany's decisions on Hanna. She worked with kids, after all, and seemed to have a certain empathy with his own child. He just never would have considered that she'd care one way or another about those effects on him.

Certain her sympathy toward him would dissolve with what he was about to tell her, and unwilling to let her any further into territory he'd declared off-limits even to himself, he allowed only minor corrections of facts.

"Tiffany is my ex-wife. And it's been five months since she sent Hanna back. I'm just glad she's home.

"I should have taken you into town hours ago," he continued, anything but subtle about the change of subject, "but it's pouring rain out there and I'm dead on my feet." Certain she wasn't going to like what he'd arbitrarily decided, he braced himself for attitude. "It's a forty-mile round trip into town and back, and I don't want to fall asleep at the wheel. It'll be best if you stay the night. I'll take you into town first thing in the morning."

Sophie blinked at him. Disbelief held her tongue. From the moment he'd made it clear he had no interest in calling her uncle that evening, she'd been sure she'd have to explain why her uncle wanted him to call—which meant she'd have to tell him why she needed temporary asylum, and ask for that refuge herself.

Excuse me, but I got myself kicked out of my country and I don't have anywhere else to stay just now.

Pathetic and irresponsible as that sounded, she would have had little choice but to swallow her pride and do just that. But with his pronouncement, she didn't even need to mention her conversation with her aunt—or that he was to call her uncle—until tomorrow. After he was rested.

It was all she could do not to sigh in relief. "Of course." She released the words in a rush. "I can sleep on the trundle bed in Hanna's room."

"That won't be necessary." A little wary of how easily she'd capitulated, he slowly uncrossed his arms. After the displeasure she had shown when she'd learned her original plans had been altered and other arrangements made for her, he'd expected at least a little grief about yet another change. Not that it would have mattered. He was going to bed.

Just grateful that he didn't have to talk her into anything, since his coaxing skills where women were concerned were beyond rusty, he tipped his head toward the hall. "You can use the room Angie stayed in."

"Angie?"

"The housekeeper. It's the room next to Hanna's."

"I'll get my bags."

"No need." He flipped off the lamp on the desk, reached for the switch by the doors. With the flick of his finger, the room went dim. "They're already in the room.

"I know Angie changed the sheets in there before she left," he continued, leaving her to follow him past the dim, bare living room. "There are clean towels in the closet in the bathroom." Since she'd helped Hanna wash up, she already knew where that room was. "Help yourself to whatever you need."

She followed him around the corner, their footsteps muffled by the taupe carpet running the length of the long hallway. "May I use the phone?" If he wasn't going to call her uncle, she needed to. Preferably before her aunt started to worry and one of them called and woke him up.

"There's one in your room."

He stopped by the open door next to Hanna's partially closed one. Though the light wasn't on inside the room he'd assigned her, in the light of the hallway, she could see her bags sitting just inside the door.

When he turned, she could also see that he was unbuttoning his shirt.

"I'm going to say good-night now," he said, his voice quiet in deference to his sleeping child. "Morning comes early, and I need a shower."

She already saw him as powerfully self-contained; a commanding, demanding man relentlessly pushing his own limits. Watching his fingers slip buttons from their holes, that impression was joined by an image of rock solid muscle, naked under running water.

That wholly unnerving mental picture made it difficult for her to meet his eyes. As it was, she looked from the breadth of his chest to the streak of dirt bisecting his cheek. That smudge ended by the faint white scar at the corner of his beautiful mouth.

She should not have found him at all appealing. He did need a shower. Badly. Standing closer to him now than she had in the den, she could see a film of dirt along one side of his strong neck. He smelled of sweat and hard work. And of something indefinably, intrinsically male.

Feeling more out of her element by the moment, she curled her fingers around the quarter-sized jacket button at the base of her throat. "Rest well."

His eyes held hers, making her heart beat a little too quickly before his glance dropped to her mouth. When it fell to the fist at the base of her throat, his jaw seemed to harden.

"See you in the morning," he finally replied, and left her to duck into her room seconds before he turned out the light at the end of the hall.

Chapter Four

The rain let up a little after four o'clock in the morning. Sophie had listened to its beat on the roof, hoping the sound of it would lull her back to sleep. Instead, it seemed to quit altogether.

Half an hour later, with her body clock still on Valdovian time and her racing mind making sleep impossible, she was up, dressed and quietly on her way to the kitchen to make tea with the box and tea ball in her hand. With a cup of the soothing hot liquid, she could pace and ponder as well as sit and stew about her host's potential response to keeping her on as a temporary houseguest.

The rich scent of coffee reached her as she turned from the hall and passed the den. The kitchen lights were on. Their bright glow spilled toward her, illuminating the polished hardwood floor and the wainscoting on the wall to her left. Shadows stretched across the bare dining room to her right.

She could hear no sound, though, other than the gurgle of a coffeemaker.

Wondering if Carter had put on his coffee then returned to his room, she cautiously stepped inside the doorway.

Carter was there.

He stood at the sink, his back to her. With his head lowered and his arms spread wide on the edge of black granite, it seemed his fatigue last night needed more to cure it than whatever sleep he'd had.

As hard as she suspected he worked, she didn't doubt that he was still tired. Yet, as she watched his broad back rise with a deep breath, what she could see seemed to be more than a need for time to fully waken. There was weariness in the way he stood there, something that made his wide shoulders sag beneath its weight. He looked worn down, defeated, like a man drained not so much of energy but of purpose. That fatigue seemed to reach beyond his body and into his very soul.

What she sensed in him disturbed her. So did the realization that she shouldn't be in this room. She was invading his privacy as surely as if she'd just pried open a diary.

Holding her breath, she started to step back.

As if sensing her presence, his whole body straightened and he turned before she could escape.

He hadn't buttoned his shirt. Or put an insulating one on under it. He'd taken time only to throw the flannel on over his jeans, which he hadn't bothered to snap or buckle. Above the mercifully closed zipper, an inverted chevron of dark hair dipped below worn denim.

Her pulse skipped. Realizing she was now staring at a wall of corrugated abdominal muscles, she pulled her glance past well-developed pectorals and found her gaze stalled on his.

Any impression of dejection she might have had about him vanished like ash blown by wind. Having drawn to his full height, his smoky gray eyes held hers, pinning her where she stood in the doorway.

She was twenty-nine years old, well educated and possessed what she considered adequate knowledge about men and sex. In theory, if not in practice. But she'd never simply looked at a man, had him look back and felt her entire body go warm.

More intrigued by the phenomenon than she should admit, equally disconcerted by it, she dropped her focus to his feet.

They were bare.

"I didn't mean to intrude…"

"You didn't." He spoke quietly, his deep voice rough from sleep. As if daring her to conclude otherwise, he muttered, "I'm just waiting for the coffee."

Carter watched her lift her chin, give him an uneasy little smile. She'd clipped her hair neatly at the nape of her neck. If she was wearing makeup, it was too subtle for him to notice anything other than the freshness of her peaches and cream skin and the darkness of her long lashes. Her eyes betrayed her, though. It was as clear as the chips of amber in those guarded brown depths that she wasn't comfortable with his state of dress.

They were even. He wasn't comfortable with hers, either. The understated, clearly expensive, toffee-colored turtleneck sweater she'd tucked into matching slacks covered her modestly from neck to wrist. It also skimmed her narrow ribcage and the tantalizing roundness of her small breasts. A thin, bronze-colored belt defined a waist nearly narrow enough for him to span with both hands.

The thought of feeling her firm flesh beneath his palms had his body going tight as his glance dropped the length of her narrow slacks, skimming her slim hips, her long legs. The flats she wore revealed her to be shorter than he'd thought she was. He'd have preferred her in the impractical heels she'd worn yesterday. Without them and the boxy jacket that had hidden most of her feminine shape, she looked smaller, far too tempting and oddly vulnerable.

She so clearly did not belong in his kitchen.

The coffeemaker sputtered to silence.

Opening the cupboard behind him, he pulled out a heavy ceramic mug. "You drink coffee?"

"Not normally," she replied, sounding as if she would, though, to be polite.

"What would you rather have?"

Lifting her hand, she held up a small green box. "Tea. If you don't mind."

Brown ceramic clinked against black granite. "Where'd you get that?"

"I brought it. I didn't know if the kind I like would be available in such a remote place."

He looked from her French-manicured hand. They were remote, but it wasn't as if Montana was on another planet. Between the Internet and the post office, they could get just about anything. Eventually. "What kind is it?"

"Decaffeinated organic green. It's loaded with antioxidants," she said, as if that was a good thing. "Would you like some? I have another box."

Her quick generosity had him murmuring an equally unhesitant, "Thanks, but I wouldn't want to cut into your stash." He slid the pot from the coffee maker. "You go ahead."

He preferred something heavy on the caffeine, anyway. Usually because he needed it to clear the cobwebs from his brain and his body needed the charge. When he'd dragged himself from bed that morning, though, his mind had been disturbingly clear. His faults and failings had all been right there, demanding attention when there was little he could do about any of them.

"Would you mind if I boil some water?"

Shoving the unwanted thoughts aside once more, Carter motioned toward the lower cabinets by the stove. "Pots are on the right. Unless you want to use the microwave."

It occurred to him, vaguely, that she probably already knew her way around his kitchen. When he'd come in last night, he'd noticed that she'd washed the dishes that had been in the sink and put them away. She would have fed Hanna. She'd even folded the clothes he'd left on the table.

"The microwave is fine. If I may get a mug?"

He occupied the front of the sink, an arm's length from the cabinet that held what she needed. From the way she remained rooted where she was, it seemed she found his proximity to her destination closer than she was comfortable with. Her glance moved uneasily from the strip of bare chest visible between the sides of his shirt. As it did, her hand settled at the base of her throat.

He didn't know if she had any idea what it did to a man when a woman looked at him the way she did. It was the same way she'd looked at him in the hall last night; as if he disturbed her on some basic, feminine level. He'd bet his prize bull that she was as physically aware of him at that moment as he was of her.

Giving them both a break, he headed for the refrigerator, opened the door to block her from his view and pulled out a carton of eggs.

"I didn't expect you up so early."

"I'm almost always up before dawn." Relieved that he'd moved, trying not to sound it, Sophie retrieved one of his mismatched mugs from the cabinet next to where she'd found a bowl for the soup she'd heated for Hanna's lunch. Even discounting jet-lag, she'd never been one to sleep in. "I've always thought sunrises as beautiful as sunsets."

He said nothing. Preferring conversation to the silence that only made her more conscious of him, she filled the mug at the tap and carried it toward the microwave oven above the stove. "I've heard sunrises are spectacular here," she continued, as he stepped aside so she could open its door. "Do you think the weather will clear soon so I can see one?"

Carter had once preferred sunrises, too. They signaled a new day, a new beginning, new possibilities. If he had to choose now, he'd go for sunsets. At least that far into the day, the day was almost over.

Not caring for the truth in the thought, definitely not wanting to share it, he focused on the weather.

"I don't know how long you'd planned to stay, but if you're around long enough, you're likely to see a little of everything." She stepped from the stove. He moved toward it. Setting a frying pan on a burner, he turned on the heat, tossed in butter. "Some times of the year it can be seventy degrees one day and snowing the next."

"This place sounds even more untamed than it looks."

"It is untamed." He wasn't much for talking before his first full cup of coffee. But it was either talk or wonder if her skin felt as soft as it looked. "It's also unforgiving," he told her, thinking it more prudent to concentrate on the land he knew to his bones, "and rugged and intolerant of those who don't respect its ways."

She hesitated. "You don't make it seem very appealing."

"Depends on what draws a person I guess. This is a place you either love or you hate."

He didn't wait for all of the butter to melt before he cracked six eggs into the pan. After taking a loaf of bread from the pantry by the back door, he dropped four slices into the slots on the toaster. While they toasted, he grabbed orange juice from the refrigerator and poured a huge glass.

He pretty much ignored her contemplative frown. There were questions coming. He could tell by the tiny parallel lines that formed between her eyebrows. "What do you want for breakfast?" he asked, suddenly aware that self-defense had overtaken his manners.

From where she stood by one of the island's three, tall stools, Sophie eyed what he was preparing for himself. He obviously had a healthy appetite. But, then, he was a big man. It would take considerable fuel to feed all that muscle.

"Just toast, please. I can make it myself," she insisted, not wanting him, or anyone else, to wait on her. "After yours is ready."

The shrug he gave her seemed to say "Suit yourself."

"Have you always lived in Montana?"

"Pretty much," he replied, nudging at an egg with his spatula.

"Have you always lived on a ranch?"

His tone remained matter-of-fact. "Except for college."

"Didn't you want to go anywhere else?"

He reached for salt and pepper, his manner detached, his thoughts…not. There had been a time when it had honestly never occurred to him that there was anywhere else to go. But that was before the people he'd cared about most had passed on or headed for the greener pastures of bustling cities. During the years he'd spent at the university in Billings, he'd practically counted the days before spring breaks and summers when he could be back home on a horse. Paradise for him was the Mother Lode.

He'd been absolutely determined to earn his business degree, though. He'd wanted a better understanding of economics than his father had. His dad had nearly lost the ranch a couple of times because he'd had nothing but the land to fall back on when hard times had hit. The ranch itself was worth millions. But selling off land to meet debt in years when beef prices were down meant less overall equity to fall back on. And every few hundred acres sold meant less rangeland to run the cattle which, in good years, paid the bills.

In a good year now, he added to his stocks—the Wall Street kind. No way would the ranch be lost on his watch.

"It wouldn't have mattered if I had."

The microwave beeped. To save her the trouble of sidestepping him, he removed her mug, set it on the edge of the island.

"Your water's ready."

As hints to change the subject went, his was apparently too subtle. Those little lines appeared again. Only now, her expression seemed more pensive than curious.

"Why wouldn't it have mattered?" she asked, sounding as if she wanted to make sure she understood. "If you'd wanted to go somewhere else, why couldn't you go?"

He nudged another egg, flipped over the first one. "Because this is home," he said, his voice flat. "I was born here. So was my brother. He was never into ranching, so after my father died, it was up to me to keep the place going." He aimed his spatula toward her mug. "You should make your tea."

With his back to her once more, he heard her move to where her steaming water waited for her.

"I'm sorry about your father," he heard her murmur. "I hope his passing wasn't recent."

Her phrasing gave him pause—until he realized what she

meant. If he'd lost his father a short time ago, the pain would still be fresh. She was hoping he wasn't having to deal with that on top of everything else.

He didn't want her thoughtfulness to matter. But it did.

"It's been ten years."

"His heart?" she asked, apparently thinking of Dave.

As far as he'd known, his dad's heart had been as strong as a bull's. "An accident with a hay baler," he told her, sparing her the details and him the memory. "And thanks."

"Your mother…"

"Died when I was eight. Apparently there were complications when Drew…my brother," he clarified, "was born." Having gone as far as he cared to go with his past, he brushed the unwelcome lure of her concern aside. "Do you need a spoon or anything?"

He took it for granted that most women were born curious. They were like inquisitive cats who innately poked and prodded at whatever had their interest until their interest was satisfied or they grew bored enough to move on. Yet, until less than twenty-four hours ago, he'd never met a single female who could so consistently bump into the parts of his life he'd rather not talk about at all.

His younger brother had never taken to ranching. He'd pretty much hated everything about it, in fact, and had hardly been able to wait to leave for college. He'd wanted a law degree. He'd wanted a house on the ocean. He'd wanted a sailboat. He'd wanted his inheritance after their father had died in cash, not land. He now had all that and more in San Diego, part of it financed by stock dividend checks from Carter. It had taken Carter years of shrewd investing to pay off Drew's half of the ranch and all that had come with it, but the Mother Lode now belonged solely to him.

Though he and his brother had next to nothing in common, they were still brothers. But Tiffany ultimately hadn't wanted anything to do with the ranch, either.

With the abruptness of a door slammed by the kick of a boot, he closed off the thought. None of what was going through his head would have occurred to him now if not for his guest's little game of twenty questions. Determined to make sure he changed the subject completely this time, he turned to find her looking at him with something that looked suspiciously like sympathy.

"I didn't mean to get so personal," she said before he could say a word. The apology in her eyes slipped into her voice. "I didn't realize this was your ancestral home. From what you said, I thought there might have been something else you'd wanted to do. But I understand that some people are born to carry on, so I can see how duty would keep you here."

His knee jerk response was to inform her that far more than duty made him stay. Yet, even as he opened his mouth he realized that she, this stranger he would swear didn't know a cow chute from a combine, somehow understood what his brother and his ex-wife had never been able to get.

This life ran in his blood. It was what he wanted. Yet duty did bind him to this land. His father and his grandfather had loved this place as much as he loved it himself, and it was his responsibility to keep it prospering. It was just that, deep down, he no longer knew what he was working so hard for. With no sons and a daughter who showed no interest at all in what she'd need to love to run a ranch, he had no idea what would happen to the land after he was gone.

The soft pats of little feet on the floor spared him further pointless admissions.

Hanna wandered through the doorway. With her bare toes

peeking from the hem of her pink rosebud-covered night-gown, she rubbed her eyes with her fists while she yawned her way into his arms.

She gave him a sleepy little smile as he lifted her up.

"Mornin', punkin'," he murmured, resolutely back to priorities.

"Mornin'," she softly echoed.

Morning was his favorite time of day with his daughter; the only real time he'd had with her in what seemed like weeks. As she rubbed her eyes, he cupped his hand to the back of her head, nudging it to his shoulder. Their little ritual was for him to carry her to the island, where he'd prop her on the edge while he stood there drinking his coffee and she woke up.

His back remained to the woman who'd finally gone silent. Hanna's forehead rested against the side of his neck. Her eyes must have stayed open. The moment he turned, he felt the slackness fade from her little body.

The child who normally said little before breakfast, jerked up her head and gave a little gasp.

"Sophie!" she squealed. "You're still here!"

She slipped from his arms as if she'd been greased. Her bare feet hit the floor. Arms outstretched, she launched herself toward the woman breaking into a smile and wrapped herself around Sophie's waist.

Looking a little startled by her enthusiasm, but graciously welcoming it, Sophie set her back, leaned down and smoothed her sleep-tousled hair from her eyes.

"Did you sleep well?" she asked.

Swiping back a handful of her wispy hair herself, Hanna nodded. "I dreamed."

"You did? About what?"

"I floated on my tip-toes."

Sophie lifted her chin, gave a knowing nod. "You were a ballerina."

Conscious of the big male towering over them both, Sophie rose. With her hand on Hanna's head, she absently stroked the child's long, baby-fine blond hair.

"We worked on the five basic positions yesterday," she explained. "They must have been on her mind when she fell asleep."

From the sharp withdrawal she'd sensed in him, she feared she'd overstepped herself a few moments ago. She just wasn't quite sure what she'd done. He'd answered her questions easily enough. He'd even offered more than she'd asked. Still conscious of her thoughts of escape yesterday, and of the impression of isolation and weariness about him when she'd first walked in, all she'd wanted was to understand why he'd chosen to live the life he had.

If there was anything she understood it was duty, which was why she now realized why he'd struck her as being such a force unto himself. He had to be. With his family all but gone, he'd been left bearing its standard alone.

Hanna moved to her father, cranked back her neck to look up at him. "Sophie showed me how to whistle with my thumbs."

Carter's right eyebrow lifted. "She showed you how to whistle?"

Hanna's head bobbed.

"Did you learn how?" he asked.

"Only sort of," she admitted quietly. Her little nose screwed up. "I can't get loud like Sophie."

Carter's eyebrow rose higher. The woman seemed to epitomize the word "lady." The thought that she knew how to whistle in such a manner seemed totally incongruous to him, completely inconsistent with her otherwise serene, almost dignified manner.

"Where did you learn how to do that?" he asked.

"On a sheep ranch in Spain. They train their herding dogs commands by whistling. I asked the trainer how he did it and he showed me." Much to the chagrin of her mother, she remembered, who happened to later catch her in what she'd thought was a deserted hedgerow, practicing as she'd strolled. The Princess Royal had promptly informed her that a proper lady, much more so a proper royal, did not make such a piercing noise, especially in such a crude manner.

"You were on a sheep ranch?"

"Only for an afternoon." There'd been a state dinner to attend that evening at the palace in Madrid where their little entourage had stayed. She'd been included in an effort to see where she might best serve the crown. She'd been twenty-one at the time. They'd gone as part of a tour to help boost economic development.

Considering her recent gaffe over the tulip bulbs, it seemed the economy still was not her forte. At least in Spain, no one other than her mother had seen her.

Carter opened his mouth, promptly closed it. He wanted to know why she'd been on a sheep ranch. He wanted to know what had prompted her to teach his daughter such a skill, valuable as it could actually be where they lived. What he wanted most, however, was not to be that curious about her.

"Come on," he said to Hanna, lifting her up to set her on an end stool at the island. Opposite her sat Sophie's cooling mug, the small green box and a mesh ball on a little chain. "I'll get your milk."

"Can I have tea?"

His brow pleated. "You don't drink tea."

"Uh-huh," she said. "I like it."

"She had tea with me yesterday. There's no caffeine in this kind," Sophie reminded him. "But I did add a pinch of sugar."

The look he gave her was totally unreadable. He said nothing, though. He just turned his attention back to his daughter.

"Some other time," he told her. "For breakfast, you need milk."

Intent on getting on with his morning, Carter headed back to the refrigerator, moving his eggs from the heat on the way. He was aware of Sophie behind him as soon as he'd vacated the area by the island, but he didn't so much as glance toward her as he poured cereal into a bowl and set it in front of Hanna.

He had the sense as she steeped her tea and Hanna dawdled with her corn puffs that there was something more she wanted to say. Or, more likely, to ask. Some other question that would lead somewhere else he didn't want to go. At least with Hanna there, she kept whatever it was to herself.

Just to be sure she kept it that way, he buried his nose in a two-day old newspaper he hadn't had time yet to read.

He heard her set her ball in the sink.

Now that she had her tea, he was hoping she'd take it to her room and leave them to what was left of their routine when Hanna suddenly slid from the stool. He called after her to get her slippers as she raced past the dining room, her bare feet slapping on the floor, and turned down the hall. He'd barely had time to wonder what she was up to when she returned dutifully wearing her furry kitty slippers and carrying a snow globe.

She wanted Sophie to see it. Why she didn't say, but it

seemed terribly important to her that the woman who set aside her mug to take the toy know that it played music if the lever on the bottom was turned, and that she could make it "snow" by turning it upside down.

He'd wolfed down most of his breakfast at the island and was about to tell Hanna she needed to finish hers when she disappeared again in the blur of blond hair and pink rosebuds. When she returned this time, she brought her hair brush and a wide barrette.

She wanted her new friend to brush her hair and clip it in back. Not up high. Low and braided above the barrette, like Sophie was wearing hers.

Paternal protectiveness jerked hard.

He knew his daughter needed feminine influence in her life. Angie, his housekeeper, had expressed concern more than once about how Hanna would follow her around, but rarely interact with her. Kate had mentioned just the other day that she'd never known a child so shy.

Hanna now stood patiently with her back to the woman who gently brushed her hair and told her she should have braided it for her last night so it wouldn't have become so tangled. Seeing how content Hanna seemed to be, he told himself he should just be grateful she was finally opening up to someone other than her dad. Yet, the last woman his daughter had bonded with had been her mother. The bewilderment and hurt Hanna had suffered being abandoned by her still felt harder on him than having been dumped by Tiffany himself.

He pushed aside the last bites of his breakfast. He would be the first to admit that the dreams that had died when Tiffany walked out had been buried long ago. They'd started their demise well before she'd even left. But the lessons he'd learned since she'd gone wouldn't be forgotten. For one thing, he'd do whatever he could to protect his daughter from ever experiencing that sense of rejection again.

He reined in the quick tension tightening his body as protectiveness gave way to logic. He had nothing to worry about with this woman, no reason to be concerned. She would be gone in a matter of hours. As for Hanna, she hadn't spent enough time with her to form any sort of real bond. He was pretty sure she was just charmed by the ballerina thing, anyway.

Relieved by the thought, he picked up his mug, drained the last of his coffee. His immediate concern had been dealt with. Operating in triage mode as he had been since Angie's departure, he didn't take time now to wonder how Hanna would get the influence she needed without forming attachments. He suspected, however, that it was one of those things he'd lie awake worrying about tonight, or wake up in the morning with it heavy on his mind.

"Can Sophie watch me today, daddy?"

Hanna looked like a little angel with her hair so neatly smoothed and clipped into place. Thinking of his own feeble attempts at pig and ponytails, he somewhat defensively watched Sophie hand the child her brush.

"I'd be happy to stay," she told him, looking oddly hopeful.

"Thanks, but that won't be necessary." It was better on a number of levels that she go. "I made arrangements yesterday with Truly. She's going to watch Hanna at her place. If you'll stay with her long enough for me to trailer Matt's horses over so I can get them stabled here, I'll ask Kate to drop off Hanna, then she can take you to the hotel."

Caution suddenly clouded her face. Hesitation marked her tone. "Will you be calling Matthew soon?"

"It's barely five o'clock. Four where he is." He was dead certain the guy didn't want to talk about his horses at that hour. "I'll call him after I get back."

The caution remained. So did the reluctance. Yet, she seemed to consciously mask her strange disquiet as she clasped her hands loosely in front of her.

It was only when he saw her fingers tighten that he realized how studied that poised posture was. It was as if the attitude of composure had been practiced into habit.

"Then, may I talk to you about something before you go?"

Considering where their conversations so far had taken him, he wasn't in any rush to get into another now. "Can it wait? I need to get dressed and down to the compound." He had forty-five minutes before sunrise. That meant he could get a horse trailer attached to a truck and, hopefully, get to loading Matt's horses by the time the sky started to lighten. "I'll stop by the cookhouse when I get back," he told her, frowning at the bang of the mudroom door. "Kate won't be leaving for town till close to eleven."

The bang was followed by a slam. By the time they'd all turned toward the sounds, the kitchen door opened, and the woman he'd just mentioned stuck her graying head inside.

"Mornin', Carter," Kate greeted. Her glance darted to Sophie. "Mornin'," she said to her, too. She didn't utter a word about her presence in his kitchen. That could only mean she knew from the time her husband got home last night that they'd come off the range too late for Carter to take her to town.

Closing out the damp chill, his sturdy, denim and sweat-shirt clad part-time cook moved straight to the business that had brought her up from the cookhouse. Whatever it was had her looking truly annoyed.

"I was going to make apple muffins for the boys that came

in from the range last night," she told him, her hands on her ample hips, "but whoever filled the order from the general store forgot the baking powder I ordered. Do you have any?"

Baking powder? "I haven't a clue. But feel free to look.

"By the way," he continued, feeling grateful for her inter- ruption as she headed for the pantry. "I'm going over to get Matt Mabry's horses and bring 'em over here after I get Hanna dressed. Sophie's going to stay with her now, but I'd appreciate it if you'd drop her off at the Scotts on your way into town and pick her up on your way back." The feed store closed at seven. Kate was usually out by seven-thirty. He should be able to be back himself when she returned a half an hour after that. "As long as you're going, maybe you could drop Sophie off at the hotel for me, too."

An absent, "No problem," came from behind the pantry door. "I'll stop and pick up baking powder, too. I'm not seeing any in here." Exasperation turned her tone to a mumble. "Now what am I gonna make?"

The question was clearly rhetorical. Sophie, however, took a step toward the open pantry door.

"Can I help you?" she asked Kate. "If you have enough apples, I can make a tart tatin with the other ingredients."

Kate emerged from the pantry. A few more furrows had joined the creases in her brow. "A what?"

"A tart tatin," Sophie repeated.

"A tart ta-ta?" she asked, loosely mimicking Sophie's pro- nunciation. "I don't know what that is, but we don't do anything fancy around here."

"Oh, it's not fancy at all. It's what I think you'd call an apple tart. They're really quite good for breakfast."

Carter stood shaking his head. "That's not necessary."

Never one to pass up a helping hand, Kate spoke as he did.

"That sounds just fine." Any skepticism she possessed about the woman's offer, or the woman herself, gave way to practicality. For the moment, anyway. "Come on down to the cookhouse. I need breakfast on the table in an hour."

"Kate," Carter growled.

"What?" the older woman asked. "She can bring Hanna and work on her tart while I fry up sausage and hash browns."

Sophie looked to Carter. Caught between his clear desire to get her into town and her need to stay right where she was, she didn't want to say or do anything to alienate him. She could, however, show him how she could be of assistance. If he'd just let her.

"If you truly don't want me to help Kate, I won't," she assured him, all too familiar with having to bury the discouragement that came with her assistance being denied. "But there seems to be a lot to be done here for anyone willing to do it. She needs something more to feed your men. I can help her with that."

What she didn't say was how badly she ached to do something truly useful for a change. Not something ceremonial or official or assigned to her just to keep her occupied. She wanted to do something that actually needed to be done without someone else jumping to her aid to do the task for her, or have her request to help denied because a chore was deemed too difficult or beneath her. She knew respect for her position caused that deference. But her position wasn't known here, and she wanted desperately to pitch in like a normal person. Even if he didn't want her staying with his daughter beyond watching her now, his cook could use her help.

A plea she couldn't mask had entered her eyes. It remained there while she waited for him to accept or reject the offer she knew he had no logical reason to refuse.

Carter knew he had no business refusing it, either. What caught him off guard, however, was the unconcealed need in her request. He had no idea why it was there. Or why he couldn't seem to refuse it.

Already feeling like the back end of a mule because his daughter looked so disappointed, he shoved his fingers through his hair. The gesture of frustration seemed all too frequent anymore.

"Go ahead," he said, and left them all as he headed for his room to finish getting dressed.

Sophie had dressed Hanna and left with Kate by the time Carter walked back through the kitchen. He'd almost made it to the mudroom door when the phone rang.

Thinking nothing of the early call, since nearly everyone he knew was up by now, he snatched up the receiver with his usual, "Carter."

"Hey, Carter. Matt Mabry. I know it's early, but I needed to catch you before you left for the day."

"Matt. I was going to call you." About your horses, he would have said, but the man was already talking. About Sophie, who he mentioned was his niece on his wife's side.

Sophie hadn't said a word about being a relative of the Mabrys. That little error of omission, however, only compounded itself when Matt reminded him that Bree, his wife, was the daughter of a queen—which Carter soon realized, made the woman who'd all but begged him to let her help feed his men…royalty.

Chapter Five

Carter had taken Wiley Cox, his eighteen-year-old barn boy, with him to move Matt's horses. With the four thoroughbreds now stabled away from a corral of his own less pedigreed work horses, he left the lanky red-headed kid to get their feed and water and headed into the cold, his breath huffing out in a fog. A reprieve in the wet weather was the least the Fates could do for him, but he wouldn't hold his breath waiting for any celestial favors. After his conversation with Matt, he couldn't help but wonder if those same forces didn't simply have it out for him.

Sophie Saxe, indeed.

The woman was royalty; the granddaughter of a queen, the daughter of the woman next in line to the throne. A freaking *princess*.

Carter had never given any thought to the guy's loftier connections. All he'd ever cared about was that the man he saw maybe once a year shared the same philosophy he held about developers taking over range land. Matt was a Montanan himself. And a conservationist. The millions he'd made acting in movies before he'd retired had allowed him to outbid a developer for the land Matt now owned specifically to prevent more development from happening. Since the Mother Lode bordered that land, Carter felt he owed him.

Matt had just called his marker.

Carter thudded up the steps of the cookhouse, trying to remember exactly what his niece's name was. Princess Sophia Matilda Victoria Saxe-Something-er-other. Or maybe it was Victoria Mathilde. He'd written it down. Not that it mattered. What did matter was that some protocol problem she'd caused demanded that she be removed from a tiny kingdom on the other side of the Atlantic so the media in general and the paparazzi in particular couldn't make the problem worse by keeping her name and face in the press. What mattered even more was that because of whatever it was she'd done, she was now his problem. Matt had asked that he keep her on his ranch until arrangements could be made to send staff to their lodge. She would be far too vulnerable alone in a town where she knew no one, and where the shop owners and locals would be curious about a woman there on her own.

The lingering scents of coffee, bacon and sweet cinnamon greeted him as he stepped inside. Breakfast was pretty much over. Kate kept his men well fed, but even the considerable quantities of rib-sticking food she dished up in the morning took mere minutes for them to consume. Only a few of his six permanent and five seasonal hands remained at the two long tables in the open, log-walled room. At the far table, bowlegged Roy Dee sat alone nursing a cup of coffee. Farther down, Ace and Kenny, one barrel-chested, the other as skinny as a string, sat beneath the sole decoration on the golden yellow, chinked log walls; a schoolhouse clock that had hung in the same spot for as long as Carter could remember. The only other decor, beyond the pine-green plaid cafe curtains that had replaced a thirty-year-old pair of brown ones, was a rodeo calendar that had become the theme of choice after Kate had taken down a pin-up version on her and her husband's first day on the job some twenty years ago. A few of the men had grumbled about Miss March being gone, but the then-new ranch foreman's wife had made it clear it was either eye candy or her home cooking and no one had said a word since.

Ace and Kenny were talking. Both wranglers were wise-cracking to Kate, but showing company manners to the polished, brown-haired stranger taking their dishes.

Pulling off his hat, Carter left it dangling from his hand, his focus on the woman who'd been anything but up front with him about who—and what—she happened to be. She wore one of the older woman's white, butcher-style aprons over her expensively tailored slacks and sweater. Since Sophie was about half Kate's width, the bib tied at the back of her neck came nearly to the fine stitching of gold-toned thread at her throat. The ties in the middle had been looped twice around her waist and secured in the front.

It was the ease in her expression he noticed most, though. With a smile as warm as summer sunshine, she called each of the men by name as they thanked her for the apple tart. From Ace's drawled comment, they apparently didn't even mind that the apples hadn't had time to cook through.

A long pine counter separated the kitchen with its six-burner propane gas stove and long Formica counter from the dining room. From where he stopped by the commercial-sized coffee urn and platters bearing the scant leftovers of scrambled eggs, bacon, hash browns, biscuits, sausage gravy and golden, sugared tarts, he heard her tell them they were most welcome, and most generous. Looking genuinely pleased that they'd enjoyed her effort, she again gave them each that bright, unrestrained smile.

Even bowlegged, frazzle-haired old Roy, who rarely offered anything more than a grunt to anything without an engine or four legs, muttered, "You, too, ma'am," when she wished him a good day.

To Carter, she looked as out of place as a thoroughbred pulling a plow when she turned with her hands full of heavy pottery plates.

The moment her eyes met his, her smile faltered.

He didn't care at all for the way that made him feel. He just didn't bother to wonder why that was as he heard Hanna say, "Hi, Daddy," from where she stood on a chair near the metal sink.

"I rolled it," she announced.

Across the pine counter, he saw her hold up a small blob of torn, amoeba-shaped dough. Shy pride lit her face at her accomplishment.

"Sophie let me help."

She had flour on her cheek. Flour also dusted the cuff of her lavender sweatshirt and the blue dish towel someone had tied around her and pinned like a large bib to save the rest of her clothes.

Preoccupied with his daughter's new heroine, he told her it looked as if she was having a good time. Over the scrape of wooden benches against plank flooring, she assured him that she was and returned to torturing her dough.

His wranglers had a vaguely guilty look about them as they

rose from their table. Having been caught dawdling when there was so much to do, they mumbled, "Mornin', boss," and threw on their coats and hats to join the hands who'd already departed. Roy, not about to be left alone with three females, muttered his own, "Mornin'," as he followed, hitching up his pants on the way.

Kate walked up with mugs in her hands, scrutinizing the set of his face.

"Something the matter, Carter?"

"Not a thing," he replied, then motioned to the platters. "Wiley will be up for breakfast in a few minutes. Save something for him to eat, will you? I had him help me with the horses."

"I'll scramble up more eggs." Her keen eyes narrowed. "You sure there's nothing wrong?"

"I just want to talk to Sophie."

The mugs in her fists clattered to the counter. "I need to talk to you first."

"Kate, I don't have time…"

"This will save time," she insisted, and urged him toward the entry.

With her back to the cafe curtains on the door's window, and him standing in front of her, she cut a quick glance toward the kitchen. The short wall adjoining the counter blocked sight of the space where Sophie was already at work. But even with the rush of water and clatter of dishes muffling her voice, Kate lowered her tone to nearly a whisper.

"You might want to think about keeping her here, Carter. I didn't get a chance to talk to her much about her situation, but she told me herself that she doesn't want to spend what she called her "holiday" in some hotel room. She doesn't want to go home right now, either. I didn't find out why that is, or exactly where she lives," she admitted, looking disappointed at that. "We were talking about what we were cooking, then the men started showing up, so I couldn't get details. But I have the feeling a man is involved. Or was," she muttered, speculating like crazy. "A woman like that doesn't come to a place like this unless she's needing time to get her head together.

"Anyway," she went on, clearly comfortable with her conclusion. "She's a good worker. Not above any chore. I have to admit that surprised me a little, what with her being educated overseas and her family being friends with folks as wealthy as the Mabrys. And we had us a little problem with measures until I found a measuring cup that had centimeters on it along with ounces. She said she learned to cook in France and that's how they measure there. They weigh things out, too, on little scales…"

"Kate," Carter said, fairly leaking patience. Sophie had apparently given her the same evasive response about how she knew the Mabrys as she'd given him. Kate had roused his curiosity, though. It hadn't occurred to him until she mentioned it that Sophie's "protocol problem," might involve a man. Matt had made it sound as if the trouble had come from some comment she'd made. "You said this would save us time."

"It will," she promised, totally oblivious to her tendency to digress. "She's willing to pitch in with anything in the kitchen. And she's wonderful with Hanna. I really don't mind watching the child in the mornings and taking her out to Truly's, but Hanna could use some real attention…"

"I'm not leaving Hanna here with her." The situation with Sophie had changed, but his reasons for not leaving her with his daughter had not. "You just said you don't mind driving her, so the arrangements I've made are fine."

"It was just a thought," she explained, and let it go at that.

"What I'd really like, anyway," she admitted, getting to her point "is her help with the cooking. I know it's my job, but with having to cook for the extra men right now, I'm barely making it to the feed store in time for Rhonda to leave so Bill can make his shift at the Spur. I know that's not your problem, but it's causing one for Rhonda."

Rhonda Waring manned the till at the feed store in the mornings. Her husband Bill tended bar at one of the town's watering holes. Because a man overheard a lot on his stock-up trips into town, Carter also knew the couple worked different shifts so they could take turns caring for their youngsters and not have to pay a sitter. If Bill was late, he could get fired. That was Kate's concern.

Neighbors watched out for neighbors.

"Besides," Kate hurried on, looking at the wall clock as if she'd just reminded herself she needed to get started on the other meals, "she wants to know how to make cowboy beans and I'd like to know how to make those tarts."

As long as people weren't crossing his personal boundaries, Carter usually made it a point to let people speak their piece. Now that Kate had, and having a piece of his own mind he felt a particular need to share, he let her think she'd convinced him.

"She can stay," he muttered. "I just need a few minutes with her."

In seconds, the older woman went from stunned to looking rather pleased with herself. That was about how long it took him to turn and head for the counter.

"You said you wanted to talk to me," he reminded Sophie when he reached it. She stood at the sink angled in the corner. At the sound of his voice, or maybe it was the brusqueness in it, she went still. "I think now is a good time."

The lady Kate had championed turned hesitation into a smile for his little girl as she dried her hands. He now knew what she had wanted to talk with him about before Kate had arrived at the house—which, he figured, pretty much explained the reluctance about her then, and now, as she moved past him to slip her tweed jacket over cashmere and cotton duck.

Her air of breeding was now as easy for him to understand as the polish that survived despite the incongruity of her outfit. Since Matt had said she had been more or less evicted, temporarily, anyway, from "the palace," it wasn't much of a stretch for him to assume she was accustomed to formality and servants and men bowing to her as they opened doors for her to pass. Yet, as he opened the door for her as he would any other woman, he was forced to concede that she'd given him no reason to think she expected any such treatment here. If anything she'd impressed him more with her desire to help out than to be catered to or waited on.

Not that he wanted to be impressed with anything about her. Not at the moment, anyway. Right then, he didn't much care if she was the queen herself. She was on his turf. On his turf, his rules applied. Despite her admittedly unusual circumstances, she'd done the one thing he refused to tolerate from anyone. She'd lied.

"Over there," he said as soon as they were on the porch. Motioning to the cottonwood trees separating the cookhouse from a storage shed, he let her precede him down the steps. "Your uncle called."

Beneath Carter's not-so-promising tone, the distant sound of bawling calves drifted on the cold breeze. She'd learned that the calves were being separated from their mothers for branding and a few other procedures no one had elaborated on. Her sympathy for the distressed animals, however, had been sidetracked by her own disquiet.

Since her uncle had finally reached Carter, she didn't have to bring up the matter of staying on his ranch herself. She just couldn't tell from the hard angles of his profile as they stopped near a tall and rustling tree if he'd agreed to her uncle's request, or if he'd turned him down.

Crossing her arms against the chill, she watched him face her, a mountain of guarded displeasure in denim and a Stetson.

Diplomacy seemed to be in order, which meant she would not point out that she had asked him to call her uncle. Twice. Or that she'd tried a while ago to talk to him about this herself.

"I'm sorry Uncle Matthew couldn't reach you last night," she hurriedly began. "I don't know if he told you or not, but he tried to reach you a couple of times before you returned. I'd planned to present our request myself when you got in. And I would have," she stressed, "but once you said I needed to stay, there didn't seem to be any point in asking if I could. Last night, anyway."

He made her nervous. That was as obvious to Carter as the consternation her usual poise couldn't seem to mask. He didn't want her feeling intimidated on his account. All he wanted was make sure they understood each other. Specifically, that she understood him.

"It's not whether I'd learned last night or this morning that bothers me. What bothers me," he emphasized, "is that you could have been a lot more up front with me before I'd left yesterday. I can handle just about anything but someone lying to me.

"Under the circumstances," he conceded, even as her mouth flew open, "I suppose I can see why you weren't in any rush to tell me who you really are. But if you're going to stay here, you're going to have to be honest with me. I ask a question. I get a straight answer."

Sophie's mouth snapped shut. While she appreciated his concession, she didn't care at all for his approach. With her fate in his very capable-looking hands, however, she bit back her offense at his accusation. Tried to, anyway. She'd never been accused of lying before.

"I didn't lie to you," she insisted, that offense leaking out nonetheless. "I may have omitted a few details and not denied what you assumed, but I didn't lie."

"Those assumptions," he insisted right back, "were what led me to believe I could trust you with my daughter."

"You *can* trust me. Just because I didn't give you my title doesn't change anything else I told you. Every word I said was true. And I didn't tell you who I am or why I'm here because, until I talked to my aunt and uncle, I didn't know if I could trust *you*."

Their voices were still low, but her emphasis on her last word made it clear to her that her calm had definitely slipped. They were practically toe to boot. Which one of them had moved forward, she wasn't sure. She was quite certain, however, that she didn't much care for the way he stood towering over her, his hands jammed on his hips and looking no more willing than she felt to back down.

Realizing she was getting royally peeved at his male posturing—and actually letting it show, she pulled her eyes from where they'd locked on his.

Totally disconcerted, she tightened her arms over her jacket and apron and took a step back.

Carter saw the animated spark in her eyes dim, watched it fade completely under a cloak of forced composure. The phenomenon had him going silent. It annoyed the daylights out of him that she had a point about not knowing if she could trust him, either. Now, having glimpsed the spirit beneath the polish, he felt oddly cheated by the quick change in her manner. And a little uncomfortable with his own.

She was now his guest. Even if he hadn't felt a certain allegiance to Matt, his basic sense of decency wouldn't have allowed him to refuse the man's request. It didn't matter that he wasn't at all comfortable with her insights about him, with his daughter's attraction to her, or with how her quietly seductive presence taunted physical needs long ignored. As Matt had said, the woman was alone. She was vulnerable. Even if she hadn't been royalty hiding out from the media, she'd need someone to look out for her. She was in an unfamiliar place with no one else she could turn to for help.

He drew his hand down his face, blew out a long breath. It wasn't enough that he'd spent the past five months trying to figure out what to do for his sweetly feminine, definitely girly almost five-year-old. What in the hell was he supposed to do with a princess?

The only thing he could do, he supposed, was take care of her. Being a practical man, that meant her safety came first. And that meant he needed her cooperation.

"Your uncle said it could take them a week to get temporary staff in for the Bauers."

A week. Seven days. One hundred sixty-eight hours. Give or take.

He hoped he hadn't made the time sound as long as it felt to him. Since some of her tension seemed to ease as she tucked back a strand of breeze-loosened hair, he must have succeeded.

"That's what I understand, too," she replied, giving him no clue how she felt about the arrangement herself. He suspected her feelings on the subject didn't much matter. Matt had left him with the impression that she was at the mercy of powers far beyond any control of her own.

"Did he say how Mr. Bauer is doing?"

"All he knew was that he'd had bypass surgery," he said, putting his curiosity about what, exactly, she'd said or done to have fallen into such disfavor on hold, "and that he's hanging in there.

"Like I said, if you're going to stay here," he continued, having nothing more encouraging to offer about his neighbor, "I need you to be totally honest with me. No evasions. No vague responses that leave room for assumption or doubt. No more surprises," he concluded, figuring that should cover anything he'd missed. "Got it?"

Sophie nodded, unable to imagine anything else that might give him pause. "Got it," she murmured. "And there won't be any more surprises. I'm hardly privy to state secrets, so it's not as if I have anything particularly interesting to hide, anyway." He now knew the most exciting thing about her, what with her having been banished and all. "There's just one thing I need from you."

He hesitated. "What's that?"

"Your promise that you'll keep who I am and why I'm here between the two of us."

"I won't say anything," he assured her, his voice going tight. "But I don't make promises. A promise is nothing but words."

She'd seen the cynicism in his expression before, heard it in his voice. It had been there last night when he'd allowed what little he had about his ex-wife. She'd glimpsed it again, moments ago, when he'd said he could take anything but someone lying to him.

Sophie had no idea who else might have let him down, or if skepticism was simply his nature. Yet, while he might not put faith in another's oath, one of her aunt's comments about him on the phone last night made it apparent that he possessed his own code of honor. Her Aunt Bree had said Matthew trusted Carter because his sense of responsibility made him a breed of man he seldom met anymore; a man whose handshake was his word. Apparently, that was all the agreement there was between the two of them for Carter's care of Matthew's herd and his use of Matthew's land.

Believing her aunt, but needing stronger assurance from Carter himself, she extended her hand.

"We'll do this the way you and my uncle do business, then."

She boldly held his glance, her heart beating a little too rapidly in the moments before, unblinking, he reached toward her. She'd given him pause with her insistence, but the feel of his large, work-scarred hand engulfing hers erased any thought of why that might be.

There were calluses at the base of his fingers. She could feel them, rough against her softer palm.

"You don't have to worry," he told her, his promise in the pressure of his grip as it increased ever so slightly. "The last thing I want is for word of who you are to leak out. You'll find that most of the people around here tend to mind their own business, but if certain of them find out who you are, they'll be out here trying to get a glimpse of you. Like your uncle mentioned, next thing you know, they'll have said something to a relative somewhere else and I'll be chasing off reporters along with the coyotes."

With that, he let go and drew back.

Conscious that she hadn't broken contact first, she folded her fingers over the heat in her palm and protectively re-crossed her arms.

"As far as anyone on the ranch is concerned," he continued, his own hands back on his hips, "you're a family friend of the Mabrys and you're staying here until they can get someone else in to take care of the place and help out the Bauers. Matt said your aunt said to tell anyone who gets too nosy that you're from San Francisco, but were educated abroad, and that you work with her on fundraisers."

"Thank you for that. For your word," she clarified, though she was grateful, too, to have her new background established. Kate's questions had stretched her evasion capabilities about as far as they could go. "But reporters and the curious are only part of the reason I'd rather remain known only as a friend. I've never had an opportunity like this before. I doubt I ever will again."

"What opportunity?"

"To just be myself. I have no title here," she explained, wondering if he knew how much freedom he possessed himself. "Since no one knows who I am, that means no one has any preconceived idea of how I'm supposed to act, or what I'm supposed to do…or not do," she stressed, because the limitations were worst of all. "I'm just…Sophie. I'm grateful to just be myself for as long as I can."

His eyes narrowed. "You don't mind that you're stuck here?"

She smiled. "Oh, I wouldn't call it stuck. This is like a gift. You understand obligation and duty every bit as well as I do," she assured him. She also felt certain to her core that he sensed their oppressive weight. "You said you want to be here, but you must have felt the need to escape at times yourself. Even if just for a little while." She tipped her head, searched his strong and guarded features. "Haven't you?"

Twenty-four hours ago, Carter wouldn't have believed he had a single thing in common with this woman. After Matt's call, he would have bet the ranch that he didn't. Yet, as he considered that her title probably did come with certain responsibilities, he couldn't deny her the understanding she sought. He couldn't help but wonder, either, how repressing those responsibilities must be for her to think of exile as a gift.

"On occasion," he admitted, though thoughts of escape had never existed until a couple of years ago. "But it would just be worse any place else."

"I don't understand," she replied, clearly wanting to.

"My escape is right here." More and more, he found his own refuge simply by not thinking of the future beyond whatever tasks needed to be done. He didn't care for the thought. But knowing he could lose himself in never-ending chores tempered the tension that came with it. It seemed she'd had no means of avoidance at all. Until now.

"You're welcome to the room you slept in last night," he said, mentally backing away from her. If she could find a little refuge here, he supposed that was okay. What he didn't need was her looking at him as if she'd somehow just found a kindred spirit, or the curiosity about her he didn't have time to indulge, anyway. "And to the use of the house. Truly will feed Hanna dinner and Kate will have her back by around eight. We're working calves about a mile from here, so I'll be back by then myself."

He glanced toward the sun that had risen over the buildings behind them. "Come on." The day was wasting. "I'll see you back to Kate."

The anxiousness Sophie had felt leaving the cookhouse had decreased by half as she fell into step beside him. Yet, as she took a deep breath of air that smelled of damp earth and freedom, the compelling sense of reprieve she felt knowing she could stay and simply…be…warred with regret at having lost his trust. That had to be why he wouldn't leave Hanna with her.

She wasn't about to question his decision. She was his guest, after all. And an unwanted one at that. There were other ways she could repay his decidedly reluctant generosity.

"Kate said she always prepares lunch and dinner before she leaves," she said as they rounded the building and stopped by the steps. Lunch was packed in coolers to be taken to the men or picked up by whoever had time to come back for it. Dinner was left simmering in the cookhouse in Crock-Pots. His men helped themselves to it and cleaned up afterward. If they didn't and she found dirty dishes in the cookhouse the next morning, breakfast was oatmeal. "Do you mind if I help her with them? And with breakfasts?"

He'd pretty much already told Kate that she had herself an assistant.

"That's fine," he told her, and watched as the breeze tugged her hair across her cheek. Taunted by the way she left it there as she looked up at him, he pushed his hands into his pockets to keep from nudging it back himself. The feel of her palm against his lingered like warm velvet. "Otherwise, stay in the house. Please," he added, remembering he was ordering around royalty. "I'll call up there to check on you this afternoon."

She lifted her chin, but said nothing before he turned on his boot heel and left her staring at his back. Not that he gave her a chance to say much. Or that her silence meant anything.

That was what he wanted to believe, anyway, as he crossed the compound, nodding to the tall, long-limbed Wiley heading for his breakfast. Yet, the fact that Sophie hadn't verbally agreed to stay put nagged at him as the day wore on. There had been something about the way she'd looked at him—as if she'd heard what he'd said, but somehow hadn't cared for his plan—that had him wanting to know just what she was doing with herself.

He'd figured she was okay as long as she was with Kate. But Kate had left before noon with Hanna.

It was a little after twelve-thirty when he radioed up to the house to make sure Sophie was there.

She didn't answer.

She didn't answer a half an hour later, either.

There was still no response when he made it back to the truck again at three-fifteen.

Something told him she wasn't lolling in a bubble bath and couldn't hear the radio. Then, there was the fact that he'd told her he'd call.

Not caring at all for the idea that she was off somewhere on her own, and unable to imagine that she'd gone into town with his cook, he turned the cutting horse he'd been riding over to a wrangler and left the rest of his men on their horses separating calves from their mamas. Beneath the clouds parting to let shafts of sunlight warm this stretch of prairie, another crew led the separated calves from the huge makeshift corral to the squeeze chute where each unhappy animal was branded, inoculated and otherwise tended before being paired back up with its mom. Absently ruffling the ears of one of the herding dogs as he passed him, he jumped into his truck because it was faster than a horse and headed the mile back to the compound.

He was almost there when he noticed Matt's thoroughbreds roaming an exercise corral—and someone riding the largest, flat out, along the fence line in the distance.

Chapter Six

It didn't please Carter to know his instincts about Sophie had been right. He'd prefer not to have instincts about her all.

In the seconds before he'd bolted from his truck, he'd recognized the rider flying toward the compound on Matt's magnificent bay stallion. The clothing hadn't looked familiar, but the low ponytail billowing behind the rider's bare head had made Sophie easy enough to identify.

She was going to break her neck.

Fear for her body parts joined the need to know what in blazes she thought she was doing—and to stop the horse. A tenderfoot had no business being on an animal that size. Especially one who clearly had his head and no intention of giving it up. But even if by some miracle she could hear him yell at her to slow down over those pounding hoofs, he didn't want to spook the stallion. Or her. If she jerked the wrong way on the reins, she could turn the horse's head and they'd both go down.

She'd officially been in his charge less than eight hours. So much for keeping her safe.

A split-rail fence lined the two miles of road from the house to the cut-off that led to the two-lane highway into town. From where he moved at a jog between the circular corrals west of the main compound, he could see that fence line disappear at the rise beyond a windbreak of poplars.

It occurred to him as he tried to gauge where best to intercept horse and rider that she might have already been to the highway, since she was heading into the ranch. Suddenly aware that she was leaning into the thousand pounds of rippling horseflesh, her own head over its neck, he also realized she seemed to know exactly what she was doing.

She wasn't hanging on for dear life. She was pushing the horse as hard as he wanted to go.

The beat of his own boots slowed. His adrenaline-charged heart pounded in his chest.

His eyes narrowing on her, his stride slowed to a stop.

There was ease in the way she sat the big animal, a confidence that spoke of effortless control—and something that reminded him of pure joy as that ponytail flew in the wind.

She'd said she wanted to escape. As he watched her gallop toward the corral, he couldn't help but think that, for that moment, she had.

Willing his heart to slow, he pulled a deep breath. He did it again, jamming his hands onto his hips to watch her break away from the road and cut to the path leading through the ankle-high grass toward him. She straightened in the saddle as she did, letting the horse sense the shift in her weight, and reined in to slow him to a canter.

He didn't know if she'd seen him when she turned onto the path, or if she noticed him only now. But the abandon he'd

sensed in her moments ago had given way to something infinitely more guarded as she rode closer to where he'd stopped
in the hard pack and grass stubble between the corrals.

The old tan barn coat she wore looked familiar now. He
recognized it as one of Kate's that had been hanging in the
cookhouse by its pale blue corduroy collar. Her English-style
brown riding pants and shining black boots had to have come
from her suitcase. Considering the quality and style of what
he'd seen her wear so far, he didn't doubt there was a matching
riding jacket, velvet trimmed, possibly red, in her luggage,
too. She either hadn't wanted to risk getting it dirty, or had
realized how totally out of place she'd have looked wearing
it.

The moment she drew the horse to a halt, she folded both
reins into one hand and gripped the saddle horn. Swinging her
leg over the snorting animal's broad back, she dismounted
with the ease and grace of a dancer.

A ballerina on horseback.

The incongruous thought had his eyes pinning hers as her
feet hit the ground and she glanced up.

"How long have you been riding?"

"A couple of hours," she replied easily. "He's only the
second one I've had out. I rode the gelding first," she told him,
nodding to the chestnut calmly roaming the corral with a
smaller bay and a black roan. "He seemed the most agitated."

"I meant," he patiently clarified, "how many years."

Beneath the less than fashionable, too-large barn coat she
lifted one shoulder. "I can't remember not being able to ride.
It's jumping I really love," she confessed, her tone utterly
matter-of-fact. With the reins fisted in one hand, she reached
up and stroked the sidestepping stallion's shining neck with
her other. "These fences are pure temptation," she admitted,

"but the ground is too muddy to risk it. Especially with a horse I don't know. And with that saddle. It's bulkier than what I'm accustomed to.

"By the way," she added quietly, oblivious to having scared the holy Hades out of him, "I don't think these horses have been exercised lately. Maybe Mr. Bauer hadn't been feeling well for a while and hadn't been up to it," she offered, excusing rather than accusing. "I know you and your men have enough to do, so I'd like to take over their care while I'm here." Snagging back the strands of hair the wind had blown from her ponytail, she gave him a smile laced with concern and gratitude. "It's the least I can do to work off my room and board.

"And please don't tell me it's not necessary," she hurried on, preventing him from saying just that. "Even if you didn't need the help, I need to be with them."

Moments ago, annoyance had run neck and neck with amazement. As she pulled a piece of carrot from her pocket and he watched the animal lip the treat from her palm, annoyance now threatened to fade.

He didn't bother to ask why she wanted to be with the horses. He could see for himself as she walked past him, unlatched the gate and led her mount into the enclosure that she possessed a true affinity for the big, powerful animals. He just never would have imagined her being comfortable with something so large, or possessing the level of skill he'd witnessed.

He'd had no idea she could ride. There wasn't a shred of doubt that she could. But even as impressed as he couldn't deny being with her unexpected ability, there was still the matter of her protection and safety to consider, along with his personal peace of mind.

"Who told you these were Matt's horses?"

The gate latched with the clink of galvanized metal.

Turning to face him, Sophie tried to judge his expression beneath the shadowing brim of his hat. She didn't want to get anyone in trouble, but she wasn't going to be anything but honest with him, either.

"Wiley mentioned that he'd helped you bring over some horses this morning," she said, thinking of the lanky teenager with the rust-red hair. Somewhere around his second helping of eggs and the last piece of her tart, she'd also learned his job was working in the barn with the sick and orphaned animals. And that he was saving up for college and veterinary school. Carter had, apparently, hired him to aid that ambition. "After Kate left with Hanna, I went down to the barn and asked if he'd show me where you'd stabled them."

"I asked you to stay in the house."

"I know. But I didn't say I would," she reminded him, "and you were in such a hurry to go that I didn't get a chance to ask about seeing the horses. After Wiley showed me where they were and where the tack was, I didn't want to bother you on your radio with something I knew we could talk about later." She tipped her head, her expression as reasonable as her tone. "It's too nice out here to be closed up inside, anyway."

It was her accent that sidetracked him, that proper British way she had of pronouncing her vowels. That and the way she seemed totally undisturbed by the strands of her hair flying around her face in the breeze. The sun peeking between the billowing white clouds shot streaks of gold through what had, at first, looked like hair of ordinary brown. Those same shades of gold and umber lit the depths of brown eyes that held both hesitation and hope, and the same plea he'd seen that morning when she'd asked if he'd please let her help Kate.

She seemed to need to lend a hand. More than that, it

seemed as if she wasn't often allowed the opportunity. He wasn't at all sure why he had that feeling. He just knew he'd refused her offers a couple of times himself.

Feeling justified with his reasons for that, he focused on his barn boy.

Wiley probably had been just as enamored of the "Mabrys' friend" as some of his more seasoned men had seemed to be. The very capable young man's heart was always with the animals first, though, so she would have had to convince him she knew horses before he'd let her handle one. Once she had, Carter had the feeling the kid had been just as grateful for her help as Kate had been.

"Look," he muttered, refusing to be enamored himself. All he wanted from her was a certain amount of cooperation. On the ranch, he told his men what he wanted done and they did it. No explanations required. Even with Hanna, who tended to be very literal in her interpretations of what he said, he didn't have trouble making himself understood. Apparently, with Her Highness, he needed to elaborate.

"The reason I wanted you in the house is because I told your uncle you'd be safe here. Aside from keeping you and your identity hidden, that means I return you to him in the same condition you arrived in. No broken bones. No snakebites. No wandering off on your own, getting lost and suffering hypothermia if the temperature drops.

"I figured you'd be okay with Kate in the mornings and on your own in the house," he continued, wondering if he should ask her to repeat his concerns back to him. "But I can understand why you wouldn't want to be stuck there with nothing to do." Personally, trapped unoccupied inside four walls, he'd be climbing them. Given her circumstance, he'd concede it was possible that she'd suffer that same restlessness, too.

"If you want to help with the horses, you can help Wiley. I've already assigned their care to him," he told her, thinking the arrangement should suit her purposes just fine. "You're welcome to exercise them as long as you don't go past the cut-off road and he knows you're out there. If you want to brush them down and blanket them when you're finished, and maybe get them their feed, that would be a help, too. That'll free Wiley up to do everything else.

"Agreed?" he asked, watching her to make sure she didn't have that quietly resistant look he dismissed that morning.

He saw no resistance at all as the corners of her generous mouth curved.

She'd smiled at him before, but the look had been cautious, restrained. He'd even glimpsed the bright smile she'd given Ace, Kenny and Roy Dee. He just hadn't been prepared to be on the receiving end of that expression himself. That smile was warm, as gentle as spring rain and as she held his eyes, it felt just as renewing.

"Agreed," she said.

Disturbed by the intense need he felt for that warmth, denying it, he jerked down the brim of his hat.

"Good," he pronounced flatly. "I just want to be sure we understand each other. Are you okay out here now?"

She looked to the horses waiting to be ridden, glanced back to him. "Absolutely."

"Then check in with Wiley in an hour." The boy could take the afternoon shift with her. He'd then have Roy Dee escort her from the stables to the house. Evening and night shift, he'd take over himself. With her under Kate's watch in the mornings, his bases should be covered. "If you don't, he'll have to come looking for you."

"Won't he think it's odd that he has to keep an eye on me?"

"He'll think it odd if someone isn't watching out for you. You may know your way around a horse, but you don't know your way around here. He knows some of the Mabrys' guests have gotten themselves turned around on the roads and trails around here. He'll just be saving himself the trouble of having to help look for you later."

For a moment, Sophie said nothing. Being with the horses and having helped scrub tables, make sandwiches and peel a mountain of potatoes, carrots and onions for tonight's stew, she'd almost forgotten what an imposition she was. To this man, anyway.

From what he'd just said, he saw her as continuing to be one, too.

The bright edge on her newfound freedom lost a bit of its sheen.

"Then, I'll be sure to check in with him."

She offered the promise quietly, uncomfortably conscious of how seriously Carter took his commitment to protect her. It wasn't that she didn't appreciate the safety he offered. What bothered her as he concluded his mission with an apparently satisfied, "Thanks," and she turned to the pretty little mare dancing in anticipation of her ride was that, even here, there was no escaping who she was.

Not with him.

The thought still nagged at eight-thirty that evening as she turned down the volume on a cooking show and drew an afghan over Hanna. Beyond the den's draped, paned window the sun had set, leaving a faint glow of pink low on the otherwise black horizon. Until a few minutes ago, the child had ventured back and forth between the sofa and that window checking for the lights of her dad's pickup coming up from the compound. Tired, because it was past her bedtime and she woke so early, the last time she'd crawled onto the deep cushions she'd stayed there and fallen asleep.

It was hard not to feel disappointed again for the child. Yet, beneath Sophie's empathy an unfamiliar pleasure lingered, a kind of satisfaction she'd honestly never felt before.

She'd just had one of the best days of her life. It didn't matter that she'd had to shampoo straw dust out of her hair, that her manicure was trashed or that she'd looked infinitely less than presentable most of the day. Not a soul had cared or criticized. Certainly not Wiley or the horses, or old Roy Dee when he'd grunted, "Boss's orders," before he'd driven her up to the house. She could have walked, but he'd insisted. Had it not been for the fact that her host would prefer that she wasn't there, the day might well have been perfect.

It was just hard to enjoy her little achievement when Carter made it so clear that he didn't care for her presence. She'd bumped into that reality again when he'd reluctantly asked for her help a while ago.

At eight o'clock, Kate had dropped off Hanna on her way to the mobile home Carter provided her and Ty, along with the pair of jeans Sophie had asked her to please pick up for her so she'd have something more practical to wear. Carter had radioed the house only minutes before Kate had arrived. He'd asked Sophie to let Hanna watch television until he got there. He was towing a truck back, but wouldn't be long, he'd said, and he wanted to tuck his daughter into bed himself.

Absently brushing a bit of afghan lint from the wool slacks and sweater she'd changed into, Sophie left the den to retrieve the riding breeches she'd washed and left to dry in the long, utilitarian mud room. She'd wiped and brushed her boots, but they weren't clean enough to sit on the carpet in her closet, so she'd tucked them between the legs of the deep, metal sink.

She hadn't wanted them to be in the way. Since she didn't want anything of hers to be in Carter's way, she picked up her still damp pants from where she'd left them atop a towel on the counter at the far end of the room. She'd lay them over the chair by her quilt-covered bed. Or so she was thinking when she heard the thud of heavy boots on the outside steps.

Her heart missed a beat as the back door opened.

Carter walked in, his hat covering his lowered head and the thermal vest that had replaced his jacket hanging open over his work shirt. Seeming totally preoccupied, he shut out the cooler air and turned to the boot jack by the doorjamb.

Hooking one heel in the U at the top of the foot-long device, he anchored the back of it with the toe of his other boot and pried off the mud-caked leather. He did the same with the other. Leaving both boots leaning against the wall, he pulled off his hat and headed for the row of pegs by the door leading to the kitchen.

He had his hat on its peg, his fingers still spread across its dented crown, when he went still.

He must have sensed she was there. Remaining in profile long enough to drop his hand, he turned to where she stood ten feet away.

"Good evening," she said, wondering if this was his routine every night.

His expression inscrutable, he returned the small formality with a faint nod. "Evening."

The strong cords of his neck were visible above the open collar of his work shirt. The hard line of his jaw was shadowed with a day's growth of beard. She didn't doubt that he needed a shower. As last night, his dark hair bore a dent from his hat.

The gray threaded at his temples shone silver in the overhead light. While tonight he didn't look as if he'd been wrestling anything in the mud, she suspected his clothes still needed to go straight into the basket of dirty denim behind her.

She'd considered before that he was a very physical man. What she considered now was his physical effect on the pit of her stomach as his glance dispassionately skimmed her face, then dropped to the winter-weight garment of fleece and nylon beneath her crossed arms.

"Do you want to wash those?"

"I already did. In the sink. I wasn't sure how your machines worked," she confessed with a nod toward the washer and dryer beneath the dark window. "They're different from what I've used."

Skepticism joined speculation in his rugged features. "You do your own laundry?"

"Not usually. The laundresses take care of it," she told him, thinking of the small retinue responsible for everything from laundering the Queen's bloomers to putting a proper starch and press on miles of table linens. "But I did at university. These just don't have the same dials or knobs."

He would have assumed such a task would have been done for a princess. Even in college.

Given that the majority of his assumptions about her had taken a kick in the teeth since that morning, it seemed wiser to not take anything more about her for granted.

"Why did you do it then? At university," he said, repeating her phrasing.

"Because there weren't servants there whose job was to see it done," she said simply. "And because I didn't want to stand out from the other women by having my things sent out. Any more than I stood out already, anyway," she qualified. "I was the only student in Downing Hall at the time with a body-guard.

"For a member of the Royal Regiment, the woman blended in well enough," she conceded, hurrying on as if that detail of her life would hold little interest to him. "But I'd wanted to be as close as I could get to being an ordinary student." She shrugged as she often did, masking tension with seemingly calm indifference. "It had seemed important at the time."

It also seemed her desire for normalcy, whatever she assumed that to be, had been with her longer than he'd have thought.

Troubled by the realization, not wanting to be, he rolled up his sleeves and walked over to the sink of galvanized gray metal.

"I'll show you how to use those in the morning," he said, referring to his washer and dryer as he turned on the water. He grabbed the bar of gritty gray soap from the indented tray, worked his hands into an even grayer lather. He needed to get his daughter into bed, take a shower. "Is Hanna watching TV?"

"She fell asleep waiting for you."

At the quick pinch of his brow, Sophie nearly bit her tongue. The last thing she'd intended was to somehow sound critical of him being late again. It wasn't his fault a truck had broken down.

She knew he wanted to tend his daughter. As precious as his time with Hanna had to be to him, she wouldn't hold him up any longer. Any longer than necessary, anyway.

"I'll leave you to your evening," she said, as he pulled a dark blue towel from the wall rack to wipe his hands, "but before I do, I need to apologize. I never thanked you for letting me stay.

"I know I'm an imposition," she admitted, bluntly. Half the blame for her lapse she would take herself. The other half she placed squarely on his impossibly broad shoulders. Had he been built like a tire, or had as few teeth as Ace, or been less concerned about his daughter, his animals or keeping his word, she doubted she'd have found him anywhere near as unsettling or appealing as she did. She didn't know which count disturbed her the most, though the appeal part had a slight edge.

His heavy eyebrows had bolted into a single slash.

"You're doing this for my uncle, not for me. I know that," she told him as he hung the towel back up. "But my being an inconvenience makes what you're doing even more generous. You'll never know how much I appreciate the sanctuary you've given me, Carter. I am truly grateful for it. So…thank you."

Despite the fact that she was hugging a damp pair of pants, the nod she gave him looked quite regal. She also looked more vulnerable beneath all the aplomb than she could possibly realize.

Carter felt something distinctly uncomfortable shift inside him. It was one thing to think he'd rather not have her around. Another, entirely, to know his feelings had been so transparent that she'd felt compelled to apologize for them.

There was also something a little humbling about how graciously she accepted his less than noble attitude.

"I know you want to tuck Hanna in," she concluded, "so I won't keep you any longer. Rest well," she murmured, and started for the door.

His hand shot out as she passed him, catching her by the upper arm. Beneath his fingers, slender muscles stiffened.

"Hang on a minute," he muttered.

Vulnerability remained evident as she'd glanced up. Only now it was shadowed by a hay load of hesitation.

He wasn't sure why he'd thought her unremarkable when he'd first seen her, what it was that had made him think her feminine features only passably pretty. Every time he looked at her, it seemed he found something else pleasing about her.

What he'd noticed that afternoon was the tiny dimple that formed in her right cheek when she truly smiled.

He noticed now that it was missing.

Suddenly aware of how unconsciously he'd reached for her, he slowly dropped his hand.

As he did, her own lifted to curve over where his had been.

"The horses," he said, conscious of how she seemed to be holding in his heat. "Wiley said you put the chestnut in the far end stall."

"I did," she replied, looking as if she wasn't sure why that was a problem. "Even after their exercise, the chestnut and little bay seemed agitated. From being in a strange place, I'd imagine," she allowed, as if she could well relate to that. "They'd seemed to have a bond when they ran together around the corral, so I thought it better to keep them where they could see each other. When I took them out, they'd been in stalls on the same wall. When I put them in for the night, I put the chestnut in the end stall across from the bay."

It wasn't her rationale that concerned him.

"It was a good call."

"Then what's the matter?"

"How's your backside?"

Carter watched her mouth open. Comprehension dawning, embarrassment flickered in her eyes.

Minutes ago, Wiley had told him he'd walked into the stable early that evening to see her tugging on the bottom half of the stall door that stuck more often than not. After an especially enthusiastic yank, she'd managed to jerk the door open—and promptly land on her rump.

"It's fine." Considering the part of anatomy under discussion, she offered the assurance with an amazing amount of dignity. "Truly."

"You're sure you didn't hurt yourself?"

A hint of deep peach rose in her cheeks. "I didn't land all that hard."

She was blushing. He hadn't thought women did that anymore. Still, since she seemed to be moving easily enough, it was difficult not to smile at the thought of her pulling herself into a more respectable position. Or at the image of her brushing off her curvy little derriere while the teenager bolted down the walkway to assist her. He managed, though. Barely.

"You know Wiley would have opened the door for you, if you'd asked."

"He had plenty of his own work to do. He didn't need to take time from his chores to help me with mine."

She'd clearly claimed the job as her own. As polite as she looked about it—or maybe it was mulish, since she didn't seem to appreciate the way his lips twitched—he couldn't help but wonder just how much of that task she intended to do herself.

"Do you plan to muck the stalls, too?"

"If they need it."

"They will."

"Then, I suppose that's what I'll do."

"Have you ever mucked a stall before?"

She shook her head. "Never."

That, at least, didn't surprise him. "It's not pleasant."

"Neither is standing in a stall in need of it, I'd imagine." Undeterred by his warning, or maybe challenged by it, she added, "Whatever my uncle's horses need, I'll do."

He'd glimpsed the spirit beneath her polish that morning. It was there now, more restrained, but clearly evident in her determination. He just never would have imagined that someone wearing cashmere and smelling like sweet seduction would be so willing to shovel hay and horse manure.

More important at the moment, he'd managed to get them past the apology he hadn't been comfortable with at all.

"You need work clothes."

A bit of the obstinacy eased from her pretty face. "Kate brought me a pair of jeans. I asked her to pick them up for me while she was in town."

"Did she bring you sweatshirts?"

"I didn't ask her to buy anything else. The only American dollars I have are what my aunt handed me just before I boarded their plane. I don't think anyone thought I'd have a need for money while I was at their lodge. I can wear the barn coat Kate lent me."

"You swim in that thing. I'll see what I can dig up around here," he said, though she'd probably drown in anything he could come up with. A fleece of his would still be easier for her to move in than that bulky canvas.

"Thank you," she murmured. "I'd be grateful."

He didn't want her gratitude. Skimming her face, far too aware of her nearness, he didn't allow himself to consider what he did want, either.

She took a step away.

"One more thing," he said, keeping his hands to himself this time. His eyes narrowed. "Have you always been so headstrong?"

"Probably," she admitted with ease. "I just haven't been able to get away with it before. It's one of the tendencies I know I'm better off keeping to myself."

The flecks of gold in her eyes seemed to warm with her admission. Her unadorned mouth, however, had the bulk of his attention.

"I'll say good-night now, Carter. I didn't get Hanna ready for bed because I knew you'd want to help her. Sleep well," she added, and opened the door to the kitchen to disappear inside.

Carter caught the door before it closed, watched her pass by the island and walk through the opposite doorway as she headed for her room.

As obvious as he'd made his attitude about her presence, he'd obviously made it just as apparent that he didn't want any more help than he specifically asked for with his daughter.

The protectiveness he felt for Hanna excused that unfortunate but necessary circumstance. It also allowed him to dismiss the thought as his curiosity about Sophie kicked more firmly into place.

The woman raised more questions every time he was with her. He hadn't doubted that she was on unfamiliar ground on his ranch. Recalling what she'd said about having a laundress and a bodyguard, what he hadn't considered was how truly unfamiliar her world was to him.

Something else bothered him, too. With her soft scents lingering behind her, something that smelled of soap and herbal shampoo, he couldn't help but wonder what other tendencies she suppressed—and if, maybe, Kate had been right.

His cook had said that morning that Sophie didn't seem to be above any task. She'd proved right on that score.

She'd also said she was sure Sophie was there because of a man.

As he walked into the den to wake his daughter and he heard Sophie's door click shut in the hall, he decided that first thing in the morning, he'd ask.

Chapter Seven

Sophie's modest suite at the palace overlooked a beautifully tended topiary garden. In her sitting room, a carved marble fireplace faced a sofa of white brocade, gilded Louis XIV armchairs and a lady's writing desk. The sky-blue Venetian plaster walls of her adjoining bedroom surrounded a four-poster, damask-draped bed that had been a possession of her great-grandfather, the then King of Prussia. In her bathroom, the relatively modern plumbing had been added somewhere around 1930 and had rattled off and on ever since.

Like most members of the royal household living on the premises and not in one of the other royal residences, she chose to have breakfast in her room. A chambermaid brought her a tray with tea and toast, which, thanks to excellent satellite reception, she ate while watching the BBC or CNN.

Depending on her schedule for the day, she would dress in a suit or skirt and sweater, the latter if she would be working with small children, or in riding attire or a casual dress if the day was her own.

The room she temporarily occupied beneath Carter McLeod's roof seemed to hold history of its own. The iron double bed covered with a lovely, multicolored, handmade quilt, seemed every bit as old as the well-preserved pine dresser. An old-fashioned, trundle-type sewing machine sat near a wood rocking chair whose finish had been worn from its arms by use.

As she left her rustic little haven with her box of tea the next morning, checking to make sure the door to Carter's room at the end of the hall was closed, she'd dressed to cook cowboy beans and, eventually, to clean stalls.

She wanted to be in and out of the kitchen before he got there himself. He'd seemed marginally more approachable after her apology last night. Or maybe it was the amusement he'd tried to hide over her inelegant landing in the stables that had made him seem a bit more agreeable. Still, common sense told her that the less she disrupted his personal routine, the better chance she had of him staying that way.

She just hadn't allowed quite enough time. She realized that when he walked into the kitchen two minutes later and found her in front of the stove waiting for the microwave timer to ding.

He'd combed his thick, dark hair back from his face with his fingers. At least, it looked that way to her as she followed its slight wave to where it flowed over the collar of his plaid flannel shirt. Beneath the heavy slashes of his dark eyebrows, his silver gray eyes were unreadable.

"Mornin'," he mumbled, his voice a deep rasp as he headed in his stocking feet for the sink.

He'd buttoned his shirt. Two middle buttons, anyway.

"Good morning," she returned, grateful for that. Clothed, he merely messed with her pulse. Exposed, however partially, he had an unhealthy effect on her breathing. "I thought I'd be out of here before you got up. Give me a minute and I'll take my tea to my room as soon as the water's hot."

Carter's glance moved from the gray horseshoe embroidered on the turtleneck of her white cotton sport shirt to the pristine white socks on her feet. In between, new dark denim jeans molded her heart-shaped backside and the slender length of her legs.

It wasn't even the crack of dawn. He was barely awake. Yet he'd become instantly conscious of the grace in the long lines of her body. That fluid suppleness and the taut feel of her arm beneath his hand last night made him suspect she was far stronger than she looked.

It also made him wonder how her long, long legs would feel wrapped around his.

Any part of his body that hadn't been awake before certainly was now.

He jerked his attention to the coffeemaker. "You don't need to go to your room." He'd told her she was welcome to the use of his house while she stayed there. He hadn't said she had to hide out in it when he was around.

Figuring he must have sounded as if he'd been thinking it at the time, which he might well have been, he grabbed the carafe and filled it with water.

"I have a couple of shirts that have shrunk. I'll get them for you after breakfast."

He definitely preferred her in something baggier.

Thinking a horse blanket would work, he heard her thank him as he slipped the carafe into place. He'd just told her she didn't have to leave the room. Something about the silence coming from behind him, though, told him she planned to make herself scarce, anyway.

"Tell me something," he said, intent on preventing that. There was something he wanted know. The sooner he asked, the sooner he could stop wondering about it. "What exactly did you do to get yourself—" *kicked out of your country,* he thought "—sent away," he said instead.

Considering that he was pre-caffeine, he figured he sounded reasonably diplomatic. Wanting to stay that way, he shoveled in extra coffee just to be safe and flipped the switch to get it brewing.

She still faced the numbers counting down on the microwave. Turned from him as she was, he could see that she hadn't just pulled her hair back as she had the past couple of days. She'd woven it tightly from her crown and tucked the braid under neatly at her nape. The style looked pretty, in a severe sort of way, and practical for what he knew she had planned for the day. But mostly, to him, it made her look even more restrained when she turned to face him.

Across a dozen feet of hardwood floor, he saw that reserve merge with unease.

"Didn't Uncle Matthew tell you?"

"I want your version."

"There are no 'versions,'" she said, her brow pinching. "I said something I should have kept to myself. Anyone you ask who knows anything about it will tell you that."

That was more or less what Matt had said. He just hadn't elaborated. "Do you mind telling me what that something was?"

"Wouldn't you rather just have your coffee?"

"It won't be ready for another five minutes."

He figured he had a right to know what had landed her in his guest room. From the way her glance shied uncomfortably from his, she seemed to figure that, too.

"I just offered my opinion," she said, trying to sound

matter-of-fact, sounding embarrassed instead. "I know better than to say anything that can reflect poorly on the Crown, but I wasn't thinking. It just…slipped out."

"The Crown?"

"My grandmother. The Queen. She's the ultimate symbol of our country. Much as is your president for yours," she explained, "except family lineage grants the privileges and responsibilities rather than a public election. As a member of the royal family myself, anything I say or do reflects on her first, then on my mother, since she's next in line to the throne." Her tone dropped in obvious displeasure with herself. "Especially when I'm acting in an official capacity."

Behind her, the microwave beeped. Even more curious now, he watched her turn toward it.

"If your mother is next in line, where does that put you?"

"Oh, I'm only twelfth." The door opened with a click. "My brother will become Crown Prince when mother ascends. He already has a son and a daughter, so my oldest nephew will follow him. That nephew will then be followed by his own children or his younger sister if he doesn't have any." The door snapped closed. "If something happens to both of them before they marry and have issue, the title goes to my oldest sister, then her children, then their children.

"Or," she continued, turning with her mug of choice in hand, "to my next sister and her child and so on. The family would have to stop breeding and be pretty much wiped out before it got to me."

He looked from the white *Got Oats?* on the brown porcelain. She'd lost him after the children of her first nephew.

"How many brothers and sisters do you have?"

"One brother. Three sisters. And seven nieces and nephews

and two more on the way. Every time one of them has a child, I move farther down the list."

"Does that bother you?"

The look she gave him said he had to be joking. "The last thing I want is more opportunity to mess up in public. I do far better behind the scenes. And then, only if there isn't a camera or microphone around."

"What was it you said?"

She stepped to the island with its neat stack of coloring books and her box of tea and set the mug by the ball she'd already prepared. "That I saw no need to replace perfectly lovely flower bulbs with imported ones."

"Excuse me?"

She dunked her ball into her mug. "I was re-opening a traffic circle," she said, realizing he needed context. "I don't believe you have many of them in the western part of this country. Roundabouts, they're sometimes called. They're especially efficient when three or four roads come together, as long as there isn't a lot of traffic and you don't get stuck having to go two or three laps to get out.

"Anyway," she continued, lifting her ball to dunk it again, "this one had always had a patch of tulips in its centre. When the circle was widened, the centre was widened to accommodate a fountain and more tulips. The ribbon-cutting ceremony was to start the new fountain and dedicate it to one of our beautification groups."

She checked the color of her tea, decided to dunk more rather than let it steep. "After the ceremony, a reporter overheard one of those ladies say she'd heard the new bulbs weren't from Valdovia like the others had been. The reporter came to me and asked how I felt about that.

"He'd already asked how I felt about having doubled the

number of bulbs planted," she continued, sounding as if she thought the question one of the more inane she'd been approached with. "I'd told him the truth, that we can all use more beauty in our lives. When he stuck the microphone in my face with his other question, I told him the truth then, too. That I saw no reason to replace our perfectly lovely Valdovian bulbs with imported ones."

Still dunking, her voice fell. "I didn't know at the time that they actually were imported. They'd been a gift from the ambassador of another country."

The slow motion of the ball lifting and dropping seemed cathartic to her somehow. Or, maybe, Carter thought, as lost as she seemed to be in her thoughts, she wasn't even aware that her brew was nearly the color of grass. He couldn't believe how contrite she looked. Mostly, he couldn't comprehend how something so innocuous could warrant banishment, temporary or otherwise.

"That's the comment that got you in trouble?"

The ball fell back in, chain and all.

"They were a gift," she stressed, turning all that contrition on him. "From a country we're apparently in rather delicate negotiations with for future economic trade."

"But you said you didn't know where they'd come from."

"At the time, I didn't. But that doesn't matter. Someone in the Royal Secretary's Office should have been on top of every detail of the event and given me that information along with what I'd been given about the group being honored. It doesn't even matter that official apologies were extended because proper recognition wasn't given. Once the Ambassador made his displeasure known about how I'd dismissed his gift to the Queen, the press started digging up my other transgressions and it was easier to just make me invisible for a while.

"Look at it this way," Sophie insisted, ignoring his quick frown in her desire to make him grasp the seriousness of her gaffe. "Imagine you'd given a prized cow-calf pair to a neighbor you're in negotiations with over grazing rights. The neighbor makes an unappreciative remark about your gift. Wouldn't you be offended and no longer inclined to be generous in your dealings with him? Wouldn't *he* want to do whatever he could to erase any reminders of what had been said so you could get back to business?"

For a moment, Carter said nothing. As she stared at him in the early morning silence, a dozen more questions piled up behind those already waiting to be asked.

What transgressions? he wondered. "How do you know about cow-calf pairs?" he asked. "I thought the work you did had to do with charity and culture."

"It does. More by default than by choice. Not that I don't enjoy some of it. Especially working with children," she hurried to make clear. "I asked Wiley about how a ranch like this works. He told me about calving season and how the calf is always kept with its mother so it can eat. And about how some of the cows are shipped to market after the calves are weaned and the calves grow up to be the moms and the cycle starts all over again."

She seemed to have a handle on the bare-bones version of ranching. He however, had no idea at all what else the media could have on her.

"So what other…unacceptable," he decided to call them, "things have you done?"

Sophie hesitated.

"We have a deal," he reminded her, having no intention of letting her back out of it now. Leaning against the edge of the sink, his legs crossed at the ankles and his arms crossed over his chest, he studied the appealing lines of her face. " I ask a question. You give me a straight answer."

The agreement had seemed fair to Sophie yesterday, especially since she was getting his protection in exchange for it. She just hadn't considered at the time that there were actually a few things she'd really rather he didn't know, and impressions she'd rather he didn't have.

"That was the agreement," she murmured, though she didn't much care for the one-sidedness of it. From an information-sharing standpoint, anyway. "Just keep in mind that certain elements of our media are as rabid as yours are here. They'll dig up the most minor incidents and make them sound…"

"Major?" he offered.

"Something like that."

"So what minor things did you do?"

Compared to other royals, the more visible ten percent, anyway, her past seemed about as colorful as ash. Even taken on their own, the incidents that had disappointed or embarrassed her and her family over the years weren't all that sensational. What made them seem that way was having them all resurface at the same time. The recaps in the papers and on the Internet made it appear as if she'd been some sort of a wild child. Either that, or hideously naive.

It was the latter possibility that discomfited her the most.

"Well," she began, taking them in no particular order as she picked up a box of crayons from atop the coloring books, "by the time I left a couple of days ago, the press had reminded the public…and my family…of the only time I've ever been publicly intoxicated. I was helping a friend from school celebrate her twenty-first birthday and was photographed wading in a fountain. I had a bottle of champagne in one hand and my shoes in the other."

The photograph had been rather good actually, she thought, starting to close the box's lid. Certainly, it had been one of the more flattering taken of her. She'd never been particularly photogenic.

"Did you have all your clothes on?"

Her head snapped up. "Of course I did."

"So, what's the deal? You were having fun. You weren't naked. I don't see the problem."

She eyed him evenly. "The problem," she pointed out, "was that it wasn't dignified."

Carter opened his mouth, promptly shut it again. "Okay," he murmured sounding as if he didn't get it, but might be trying to.

"Before that, there was the time a cousin and I were trying on hats in a boutique and got the giggles…"

"Not dignified?"

"Precisely.

"But that wouldn't have been news at all if it hadn't been for photos that had appeared the week before of me and a…friend," she called him, though he'd turned out to be nothing of the sort, "on a beach in Cannes over semester break. The photos were all compromising," she admitted, "but it was the angle in one that made it so bad. The way he lay propped up on his side next to me made it look as if I wasn't wearing the top to my bathing suit." It hadn't helped that he'd been leaning to kiss her. Or that she'd had her arms around his neck.

She could practically feel Carter's quicksilver eyes moving over her. When she looked back, though, his scrutiny remained fixed on her face.

"This guy was your boyfriend?"

He was the first almost-intimate relationship she'd had.

"I'd thought of him that way," she admitted, setting the box atop the books again. Movement seemed necessary. Picking up the stack, she paced toward the table.

"He was the son of a barrister, from a good family and really quite charming. Or so I thought before I found out that he'd had a friend of his take the photos so he could get his own name into print." She set the books by Hanna's puzzle, determined to keep the hurt and humiliation from her tone. "He'd wanted to increase his prestige with his peers."

"How long ago was that?"

Carter watched her brow knit in thought as she turned. "Ten years ago. I was nineteen at the time."

He had ten years on her, he thought. Yet, he'd managed to escape betrayal far longer than she had.

At the unexpected realization, his curiosity changed quality. "I take it the press brought that up before you left."

"Along with the pictures. The *Daily Star* in London ran them Tuesday. By Wednesday, they were in the tabloids in Italy and Spain again. Another one of the London papers had a picture of me and Paolo Diego at a polo match." Swiping up a crayon from where it had fallen at the base of the island, she returned it to its box. "He was my other…mistake.

"I've only had two of that sort," she admitted. "And that one was nearly two years ago. But those particular mistakes just seem so much larger when so many people know about them. I know this will all blow over. I know someone else will do something even more stupid and this will be last week's news. But in the meantime, I get to look foolish all over again, which gave my mother the opportunity to remind me once more of what she calls my consistently poor choices in men. She makes it sound as if there's been a legion of them. There's only been two."

She came to a halt on her way past the stove, looked to where he'd remained, dominating the opposite half of the room. "I cannot believe I just said that to you."

Neither could Carter. He couldn't relate to half of what she'd just told him about the tabloids, either. He tended to ignore those lined up at the checkout counter at the grocery store, so the whole concept of an industry making people's lives miserable for profit was sort of foreign to him. He just knew it existed. What he felt fairly certain of, though, was that most women wouldn't admit to poor judgment when it came to the opposite sex. It seemed like pride would prevent it.

Unless that pride had taken a beating.

Caution entered the deep tones of his voice. "What happened with the last guy?"

"I was out of my league," she said, sticking with what was public record. "He was an international financier I'd met at a charity ball. I'd been warned that he was a playboy," she admitted, fully prepared to make a long, painful story very short. "But he'd seemed so genuine to me." Which only proved how truly naive she'd been, she thought. He'd played right into her dreams and made her believe they were his dreams, too. Only he'd never wanted children and a quiet life raising them away from the pomp and circumstance of the palace. He just wanted her to think he did because she'd proven to be such a challenge.

"He knew my position demanded utter discretion when it came to a relationship," she murmured. "He knew I couldn't get serious about anyone without the relationship being scrutinized." He'd insisted that he respected that, that he knew she had to be careful whom she trusted and that she could always trust him. He'd said all the right words. "But he hadn't really wanted me. He'd just wanted to take me to bed to see if he could.

"I'd stopped seeing him before that could happen," she confided, rather liking the fierce way Carter had frowned at her admission, "but his remarks about my being an 'ice princess' wound up in print throughout most of western Europe."

She hadn't been close enough to a man to totally trust his discretion in a relationship since. She saw no need to mention that, though. Or the fact that she could have added *virgin* before *ice* because it had become so clear to her that her lack of experience with another man was what had intrigued Paolo once he'd figured that out. That bit of information, however, was far more personal than she cared to share.

She felt exposed enough as it was. Especially when speculation joined what almost looked like sympathy in Carter's expression.

"What's an ice princess?"

Hanna's soft, sweet voice came from the doorway.

At the sound of it, more specifically at the topic of her interest, Sophie's eyes locked on Carter's.

Holding her glance, clearly unprepared for the awkward question, too, he shoved himself away from the sink.

"Mornin', punkin'." Crossing in front of Sophie, he scooped up his little girl. "How long have you been standing there?"

With her hands on both of his shoulders, both of hers rose toward her ears. "I dunno. What's an ice princess?" she repeated.

"It's ah…" Clearly struggling for something G-rated, Carter cut himself off and tried again. "It's a woman…who…"

With a smile overriding her chagrin, Sophie stepped forward. "It's a princess who's been out in the cold too long," she said, offering the first kid-friendly explanation she could think of to avoid the speculation in Carter's eyes.

She didn't want to even try to imagine what he was

thinking just then. She hadn't been describing anyone in particular. At least, she hadn't thought she was, even though she did sometimes feel as if she'd been left out in the cold herself.

The realization troubled her on a number of levels.

From her perch in her daddy's arm, Hanna murmured a quiet little, "Oh," and hugged his neck.

"You want your breakfast?" Carter asked her.

He felt her nod against his shoulder. An instant later, her head popped up.

"Then can Sophie do my hair?" Looking to the woman who'd turned to retrieve her cooling tea, she pointed to the braid at the back of her head. "Like that, please?"

Carter couldn't argue the fact that the woman with the easy smile for his daughter, and a more self-conscious one for him, did a far better job with girl-hair than he did. And no way would he even attempt what she soon identified as a tucked French braid. Still, as protective as he felt about his daughter, Hanna's hair was all he would let Sophie do for her after the child had finished her breakfast.

With that out of the way, and with Hanna standing between them in her pink nightgown and freshly woven braid, he then gave the pretty princess a hurried lesson on how to use the appliances in the mud room.

He needed to think of her as who she was. Reminding himself of her title was the best way he could think of to keep barriers in place.

The washer was working on the load of denim he'd shoved in when he said he'd dress Hanna and bring her down to the cookhouse in a while. Even if he hadn't known that Sophie wanted to be on time to help Kate, he needed to put a little distance between him and the woman he suspected could easily slip under his skin.

She was his responsibility. Because of that, the need to keep her safe felt perfectly reasonable to him. It was what he'd started to feel after he'd blithely called her on their little agreement that he wasn't so comfortable with.

She'd swallowed what had to be badly battered pride and admitted that she'd been used. Not once. But twice. And badly.

He now knew where the empathy he'd sensed in her before had come from. Whether he wanted to acknowledge it or not, it was there again. Only now, he felt that empathy for her.

He knew what she'd experienced. He knew that sense of not only having been betrayed by someone trusted, but having been betrayed by one's own judgment. He, at least, hadn't felt disgraced or dishonored. Disenchanted, certainly. But her humiliation had been far more public, then and now.

He wasn't quite sure what to make of how that offended him.

He had no trouble understanding what offended him about the men in her past, though. He knew there was a breed of male that pumped their egos by adding to the notches into their bedposts. On any given Saturday night, the Silver Spur was jammed with cowboys looking for a sweet young thing to give 'em a ride. Apparently, among the upper crust, certain of that breed felt they got extra points for a princess.

He'd never been that kind of man. Before he'd married, serial monogamy had been more his style. Since then, he hadn't run across anyone who'd done much more than tempt him. Until now. But the woman—the princess—temporarily under his care was so far off-limits to him that thinking in terms of anything other than a cold shower was pure punishment. He especially didn't want to think about her with another man.

He didn't question why that was. He just knew there was even more vulnerability than he'd seen last night beneath her polish—and that the need to keep her safe had been joined by something that felt infinitely more protective.

By that evening, all he felt was beat.

He'd spent fifteen hours working calves and troubleshooting problems that ranged from mechanical to personnel. The toll of every one of those hours seemed to hit at once when he walked back through the door, a full hour later than he had the night before.

The lights in the kitchen had been left on for him. As he headed for the light spilling from the den, the familiar fatigue wasn't bothering him nearly as much, however, as the nagging pain in his back and shoulder. One of his employees had gotten all four wheels of a quad stuck in the mud.

He hadn't asked one of the other men to help him tow it out. They'd all been busy themselves. So, he'd pulled it out himself, and pulled a muscle in the process. That was retribution, he figured, for giving the woman on the sofa reading beside his sleeping child a bad time about being stubborn herself.

Whatever Sophie had been about to say when she glanced up to see him in the doorway seemed forgotten. Eyeing the way he kneaded his shoulder, she cautiously set down her book.

Her glance swept his face, her concern appearing too quickly for her to effectively temper it. "Are you all right?"

"I'm fine," he insisted, but even he could hear the tension in his voice. "It's just a pull. It'll be better after a hot shower.

"Do me a favor, will you?" he asked, staying where he was since his need for the shower went beyond pain relief. "Help Hanna get to bed? Tell her I'll be in in a while. And if I'm later than eight o'clock from now on, just let her fall asleep in her room. It'll be easier on her if I just go in and kiss her good-night instead of getting her all awake."

"Of course," he heard her say, though her concern remained. "Is there anything else I can do?"

The request was just like her, he thought. She saw a problem, she wanted to help. But he wasn't about to ask her to get him something to eat because he hadn't had time to grab some of the supper she and Kate had left waiting for the rest of his men, or rub liniment into the strained muscle for him. The hunger in his belly was a minor annoyance. The thought of her hands on his bare skin promised more frustration than he could handle.

"The shower will do it. But thanks." With a nod caught short by a jolt of discomfort, he headed for his room before he could think too much about how appealing that quick concern of hers was. Especially when it was directed at him.

Having her put Hanna to bed at her normal bedtime hadn't been an entirely selfless request. His daughter *did* need to stick to a schedule. But in the back of his mind was the thought that it would be far easier on him if Sophie was already in her own room herself when he returned at night. To make sure she was okay after Roy Dee escorted her to the house from the stables and Wiley's watchful eye, he'd just do as he'd done earlier that evening and check in with her by radio.

That plan, however, was of no help to him at all when, his shoulder aching like a bad tooth, he found her putting on his coffee for him the next morning.

Chapter Eight

Sophie finished filling Carter's coffeemaker and flipped the switch as she'd seen him do the past couple of mornings. Taking his mug from the cupboard, the heavy brown one he seemed to prefer, she set it beside the pot, then headed for the desk to leave him a note.

She hadn't seen him after she'd tucked Hanna in for him last night. Because he'd said he would, she felt certain he'd gone in to kiss his daughter after he'd cleaned up, but she hadn't heard him in the hall, even though she found herself listening for him. It seemed to her that a man his size should make more noise when he moved around. But when he wasn't wearing his big boots, she could barely hear him at all.

"You didn't have to do that."

Her heart jumped in her chest. Her hand splayed over it. Far more concerned with the tightness in Carter's voice than the start he'd given her, she turned from the desk to face his frown.

He'd stopped on the kitchen side of the island, not far from where his coffee had just started to drip.

He looked terrible. The lines fanning from the corners of his eyes appeared even deeper than they had the night before. The way he'd finger-combed his dark hair made it look as if he'd missed half of it.

What had the bulk of her attention was the way his right hand gripped the muscle between his neck and shoulder on the opposite side.

"I was up and you weren't," she said, assuming he was referring to her having given him a jump start with his caffeine. "I thought I'd put it on before I left so you wouldn't have to wait for it."

"You're leaving this early?" Carefully, he tipped his head to one side to stretch the muscle. He promptly winced and straightened back up.

At his obvious discomfort, she turned from the desk with its CB radio and stacks of magazines and mail. "Kate's going to pick me up on her way to the cookhouse. I was about to leave you a note and ask you to bring Hanna's brush and some ribbons when you bring her down. I can do her hair there." Without waiting for him to decide how he felt about that, she nodded to what he kneaded. "Your shoulder isn't any better?"

"It's fine." Apparently realizing he'd growled the claim, he tempered the edge on his tone as much as he could. "Thanks for the coffee."

"You're welcome. And by the way," she said blandly, "you're a terrible liar.

"You said I had to be straightforward with you," she reminded him, when he seemed to take offense at that. "Since you insist that I have to be completely up front, I think you could at least be marginally honest with me."

Her conclusion was offered with the unwittingly regal arch of one eyebrow.

His response was to knit his own more firmly together and mutter, "Fine. In that case, it hurts like a sonofab…gun."

His verbal save had been narrow, but at least now, he wasn't insulting her intelligence.

"Have you taken an anti-inflammatory?"

"Not since last night."

She'd seen ibuprofen in the cupboard by the sink. Turning toward it, she picked up the large bottle and held it up. "Is this what you take?"

"Yeah," he murmured. "That's it."

"Hold out your hand."

She asked how many tablets he wanted, shook them into his broad and callused palm. Remembering the rough feel of those calluses against her palm, even more conscious of the remembered heat and strength, she grabbed a glass, filled it with water and handed it to him.

The corded muscles in his neck convulsed as he swallowed the pills. Aware of how close she stood, she took a step back and waited for him to set the glass down.

"Thanks," he said again, and promptly dug his fingers back into the sore spot.

"Have you rubbed anything into your shoulder?"

"I can't reach where it needs to go."

She eyed him evenly. She was standing right there. She had two good hands. She also, suddenly, had nerves fluttering in her stomach.

"Do you want me to rub it in?" The man was in pain. Considering all he had done for her, all he was still doing, helping ease that pain was the very least she could do. "If I put a warm compress on it afterwards, you might lose your scowl before Hanna wakes up."

That scowl only deepened as Carter weighed the merits of her offer against the consequences of refusing it.

He'd had a miserable night. He had another long day ahead of him and too much to do to be handicapped by a pulled trapezius and pride. Self-preservation also played into his hesitation, but he knew he'd be in worse shape in a few hours if he turned her down.

Thinking only of the ache, he told her he'd be right back.

Refusing to think about what she'd just offered to do, Sophie told him she would get a clean hand towel for the compress and followed him as far as Hanna's bathroom. She had the blue terrycloth she'd taken from the linen closet lying on the island by the bowl of fruit she'd brought up from the cookhouse when he walked back in.

"I appreciate this," Carter muttered, and handed her a half-used tube of sports cream.

Sophie stared at the crumpled tube. It was the giant, economy size. "So…" she began, gamely scanning the heavy blue fabric covering his shoulder. "Where do you want this?"

He hadn't buttoned his shirt. Opening the sides as he faced her, he eased out his left arm, grimacing as he did, and dropped the shirt on top of the towel.

Sophie's breathing grew shallow.

He was a big man. Tall, powerfully built. She just hadn't realized how powerfully until she found herself an arm's length from the corrugated abs and beautifully developed pectorals she'd glimpsed her first morning there.

His arms were roped with sinew and muscle. So was his broad back when he turned.

"By my left shoulder blade," he said, sounding as tense as

she suddenly felt. As if he knew it would be easier for her to get to the sore spots if she didn't have to reach, he snagged the bottom rung of the nearest stool with his foot, tugged it closer and sat down. "Up to my shoulder."

Sophie swallowed. Hard. Thinking that was a lot of area to cover, she squeezed a generous line of the analgesic onto her fingers. The strong scents of camphor and eucalyptus blended with his soap and brewing coffee as she touched her fingers to the side of his spine.

"How did you hurt yourself?"

"Pulling a…"

His voice cut off as she slipped her fingers toward his shoulder blade. The cream felt cool to her, but his skin felt warm and slick with the balm as she rubbed little circles toward his shoulder. The muscle beneath felt as solid as stone.

"…quad out of the mud."

Her fingers tingled. Not sure if it was from the cream or from him, she told herself to think of him as she would a horse in need of salve. A rather magnificently muscled, stubborn horse.

"What's a quad?" she asked, partly because she had no idea, mostly because conversation seemed like a good idea.

"An all-terrain vehicle. We use them on parts of the range because they're faster and handier than a horse for some chores."

"And yours got stuck?"

"It's mine." His breath hissed in when she hit a particularly sore spot. "But I wasn't riding it."

"Sorry," she murmured, working more gently over the knots between his corded neck and the hard curve of his arm. Cement had more yield.

She needed him to keep talking, to get him to relax. "Who was?"

"One of the new guys we hired for roundup. The kid had references as a good roper, but he is a show-off on the quads. He has no respect for the equipment or the rules." His deep voice already held tension from the pain in his back. The edge that joined it now seemed to come courtesy of the man who'd had so little regard for his property. "This wasn't the first time he's done it."

Knots rolled like smooth pebbles beneath his skin. Tension banded his back. He carried his stress there. Especially in his neck, she realized, when she followed the line of knots toward it.

"Was he the one who got the quad stuck the day you picked me up? Someone had called you on your radio," she reminded him, easing along the rigid muscle toward his ear. "From what little I understood of what you'd said, it sounded as if someone was where he wasn't supposed to be and that something had need of a tow."

Her fingers slipped behind his ear, under his hair. As she felt the warm brush of it against the back of her hand, she wondered why he wore it so long. She rather liked that he did. It gave him the look of a warrior, of a man who cared less for convention than he did his cause. Mostly, though, she was surprised that it felt as soft as it did.

Beneath her hand, she felt the subtle shift of muscle as he slowly lowered his head. Not far. Just far enough to allow her better access to the knot she'd encountered.

He'd yet to answer her. It was hard to know if he was thinking about what she'd asked, or about the momentary relief she seemed to be giving him. Hoping it was the latter, she waited until she'd worked the knot out, then spread both hands against his shoulder. Even with both splayed she couldn't cover the breadth of the wide, heavy muscle, but she curved them over his collarbone as best she could and used her thumbs to concentrate her motions.

She heard him groan.

"That's him," Carter finally said, amazed that she'd remembered. More amazed that he could think. The deeper pressure of her hands hurt good. The lighter pressure felt like pure heaven, in a mildly tortuous sort of way.

The stronger scents of the cream had mercifully overtaken the subtle scent of her shampoo or bath soap or whatever it was that played pure havoc with his senses whenever he breathed it. With her small, soft hands on his skin, the effect of that scent on his libido, however, had remained.

"He got the engine of that one so full of mud it wouldn't run. Roy Dee has it torn down in the workshop to clean it."

"That means you're short a vehicle."

"Yeah," he sighed, easing his head down again.

"Have I met him? At the cookhouse?"

"Probably." To the right, he thought, but didn't want her to move from where she was. "His name's Dewey."

"Dewey," Sophie repeated. She remembered him. He was the only man who hadn't taken off his hat when he'd come in to eat, but had grinned at her and Kate as if dead certain of his charm. "He was the dodgy one." Kate had called him "cocky."

"Dodgy?"

"Slick. Not to be trusted."

"That's him."

"Why didn't you have him pull it out?"

"I should have. I just didn't want him screwing anything else up, so I sent him to the bunkhouse to collect his things."

"You sacked him?"

"Sacked?"

"Let him go."

Carter bit back another groan when her hands slid down and she worked her thumbs beside his shoulder blade. The heat from the ingredients in the cream had begun to penetrate his skin, loosening the knots, easing the ache. It was the heat from her skin against his that created a different sort of tension and taunted the ache he wanted badly to ignore.

It took no effort at all to imagine her hands slipping around to his chest, roaming over his stomach.

Cutting off the thought, he drew as deep a breath as his tightened back muscles would allow, slowly blew it out.

Forcing himself to concentrate on the intriguing tones of her voice, it occurred to him, vaguely, what she'd meant.

"Yeah," he murmured. "I fired him. Even if he wasn't costing me more in time and equipment than he was worth, he was causing problems for my other men. Everyone around here has to pull his own weight, and he was making work for everyone else."

She lightened the pressure of her fingers, then deepened it again.

"No wonder you seemed so stressed last night."

She spoke quietly, her voice barely audible to him as she slowly worked from the middle of his back and up the side of his neck once more.

She wasn't just rubbing the cream in, as he'd thought she would do. She was massaging the soreness out, working on muscles he hadn't even realized hurt until she eased the tension from them.

He realized, too, what else she was doing. She was actually listening to him, and understanding his frustrations. More incredibly, she was taking care of him.

He couldn't remember the last time a woman had done

that. Tiffany hadn't. Not unless she'd wanted something. His mother maybe, but whatever memories he had of her had long ago atrophied into images of whatever she'd been doing in photographs. Yet, Sophie touched him as if she cared, as if relieving his discomfort mattered to her. And she was making him ache in the process. Not just by her touch, but by reminding him of what had been missing from his life for so long, and how powerful simple caring could be.

Sophie heard him suck in his breath, saw the hard line of his jaw go harder still as his whole body went taut. She didn't know what she'd done. Or said. She did know that her thoughts had strayed. One moment, she'd concluded that he probably seldom relaxed. The next, she was thinking of how badly she wanted to be wrapped in his strong arms. A woman couldn't possibly feel cold there.

The thought of actually being held by him was enough to make her stop breathing.

She nearly did just that when he grabbed her wrist and turned on the stool to face her. That quick, decisive move put her squarely between his powerful, denim-clad thighs.

"Enough."

His low voice sounded raw. But it was the look in his eyes that threatened the strength in her knees. Something darkened those glittering gray depths. Something like need. And desire.

His glance fell to her mouth.

With her heart banging against her breastbone, he held her there with his fingers coiled around the delicate bones of her wrist. His inner thigh touched her hip. Heat pooled low in her belly as the naked need etched hard in his face seemed to flow through those burning points of contact.

She heard the quiet rush of his breath as he drew it in. Her own echoed it as her lips parted and her eyes locked on his.

The tension flowing from his body seemed to pull her toward him, even as it pushed her back.

Need vanished with the clench of his jaw. As his glance fell, he dropped her wrist as if it had turned to hot iron.

He could have tugged her forward and she would have done nothing to stop him. She didn't know which rattled her more. Realizing that herself or knowing from the way he'd looked at her before he'd turned away that he realized it, too.

She stepped back, her own voice little more than a whisper. "I'll get the compress."

"It's fine the way it is." The edge in his tone met the scrape of the stool against the floor as he rose and reached for his shirt. "You need to go. Kate's here."

The distant rumble of an engine made it past the pulse drumming in her ears. Hearing that rumble grow closer, more aware of his desire that she leave, she turned to the breakfast table and picked up one of the heavy flannel-lined work shirts he'd loaned her from the back of a chair.

Soft fabric rustled behind her as he slipped his shirt back on. Taking hers with her, desperately hoping she didn't sound as agitated as she felt, she said she'd see him in a while and let herself into the mudroom.

In her hurry, the door didn't swing fully closed behind her. She noticed that the moment she tossed her shirt over the edge of the sink and picked up one of her boots from beneath it.

From the kitchen, she could hear the sounds of coffee being poured. She had her first boot on and halfway zipped when Hanna's soft little voice followed the murmurs of Carter's infinitely deeper one.

Beyond the window, the truck chugged and rumbled to a halt. Hurrying as much to escape her embarrassment as to not leave Kate waiting, she had the second boot on and zipped and was pulling on the heavy shirt when she heard Hanna's curious, "Where's Sophie? Will she fix my braid again?"

Carter's tone sounded totally conversational to her as he told his daughter she was leaving to help Kate, and that Sophie would comb her hair for her when he took her down later.

She had the shirt on and was two steps from the back door when Hanna told her dad she wanted to show her the bunnies at the Scotts' house.

Carter's reply was that he'd like it a lot if she'd show them to him instead. He'd come get her himself tonight so she could. She didn't know what else he said. Letting herself out, she closed the outer door with a quiet click, let the storm door close on its own and hurried to where Kate sat in her truck in the pre-dawn darkness.

Confusion followed fast on her heels.

He could have kissed her. He'd been thinking about it. She felt as certain of that as she did her own disquiet. But he'd chosen to let her go. She just didn't know if that was because of who she was and what he'd promised her uncle, or if he wasn't interested because he found her lacking.

She wanted to believe it didn't matter. She would be gone soon. But that thought tore at her, too, because thinking about home only doubled the knot in her stomach. One thing she knew for certain. She was drawn to Carter in ways that could only cause her trouble, so what he'd done, or not done, was probably for the best.

In the meantime, she'd channel her restiveness into avoiding him.

Carter made that easy.

It also seemed as clear as the diamonds in her favorite tiara that what had happened in his kitchen had been of little consequence to him at all when he dropped off Hanna with her brush and ribbons. He'd given her the same nod he'd given Kate and walked out talking to Ace about a cow with a bad udder. When he radioed that evening to make sure she made it up to the house alright, he sounded as preoccupied and rushed as he always did.

That evening, true to his word to Hanna, he drove out to the Scotts' himself to pick her up and see the bunnies she'd first wanted to show Sophie. She heard him stop outside her closed door when they returned, then tell Hanna that they shouldn't disturb her as they walked on.

She'd wanted to ask how his shoulder felt. Yet, stronger than her concern was the desire to avoid the edgy awareness and disquiet she'd felt with him that morning. Both had surfaced simply hearing his voice on the radio that afternoon. They were there then just knowing he was on the other side of the wall.

She managed to miss him the next morning by being gone before he showed up in the kitchen. She could probably have avoided him that evening, too, but she had to pass on a message from her aunt.

The phone in the house also rang in the barn. She learned that when she checked in with Wiley on her way from the cookhouse to the stables and he told her Mrs. Mabry had called and wanted a call back.

Ten minutes later, having made the call in the barn's cluttered office, she left a message with the wiry young vet-to-be that she'd like to talk to Carter when he returned to the compound. Evenings definitely weren't the most optimum time to talk to him, considering how tired he tended to be. Aside from that, it seemed to her that seeing him away from the intimate confines of the house would make being with him a whole lot easier on her nervous system.

She'd left her message for him over six hours ago.

Trying not to think about the time, she worked the curry brush over the chestnut-colored coat of her uncle's pretty bay mare. She had the elegant thoroughbred cross-tied between the uprights of two stalls. His other horses roamed a fenced pasture beyond the compound, either having been groomed yesterday or awaiting their turn for her attention tomorrow.

The radio playing softly from the tack room was tuned to a channel that identified itself as "playin' the best country-western music in all of Big Sky Country."

Sophie wasn't familiar with the songs, but like her new routine, the music had grown on her. In the lyrics, the men sounded strong; the women stronger. Or, at least, as if they were trying to be. Or would be, as the female voice drifting on the cool hay-and horse-scented air currently lamented, if it weren't for men.

She'd worked up a fine layer of dust from the mare's short hair when she suddenly went still.

The sun had finally won out over the clouds. A long beam of its light stretched halfway down the wide walkway of the stable. From the corner of her eye, she caught sight of a long, imposing shadow down by the wide, open doors.

Carter saw her head come up, noticed her quick hesitation. Like a mare scenting a stallion, a certain caution seemed to fill her entire body before she glanced toward him. In the sunlight radiating from behind him, bits of dirt and hay dust in the air glowed like flecks of gold. Facing that light as she was, he doubted she could see the guard in his own expression.

That guard was there, though, right along with all the reasons he needed to keep his hands to himself. He couldn't believe how close he'd come to ending his curiosity about how soft her tempting mouth would feel.

The hollow thud of his boots on the floorboards joined the low sounds of the radio. He thought nothing of her taste in music. In these parts, on that particular radio, country-western was her only choice.

His silhouette became substance as he walked toward her, his hat pulled low, his stride easy. Sophie knew his shoulder still bothered him. Kate had mentioned seeing him rub it that morning and had wondered aloud what he'd done to himself. Sophie hadn't mentioned the quad, or that she knew exactly how tight all that magnificent muscle had been.

Beside her, the mare's head had come up, her black tipped ears twitching. Not sure who this stranger was, her tail swished as she started sidestepping from him.

"Easy, girl," he murmured, touching her withers, letting her blow on his hand. He gently stroked near the end of her long black mane. "Easy.

"Wiley said you wanted to see me," he said, his attention on the horse, his tone still quiet.

Calmed by the deep, soothing tones of his voice, the mare went still. Sensing no threat from the big man standing so relaxed beside her, she lowered her head so he could scratch between her ears.

Anything but relaxed herself, Sophie pretended otherwise.

"Aunt Bree called this morning," she said, returning to her task. She was good at pretending. In one way or another, she'd been doing it most of her life. Pretending to fit in. Pretending it didn't matter that she'd never felt she had. "I can probably be out of your hair in a few days."

The usually buried thought made her smile feel strained as his glance slid to her.

She wore the navy blue sweatshirt he'd loaned her. She'd rolled the sleeves to her elbows. The hem hit mid-thigh. He'd told her it had shrunk. Had it still fit him, it would have reached her knees.

"Probably?" he asked, giving no hint how he felt about that.

"She said that finding trustworthy, live-in temporary help on short notice is a challenge, but they're verifying references on a couple of people now." She didn't mention that her aunt had also wanted to make sure she was still comfortable staying with him. There being various definitions of "comfort," Sophie had chosen the response least likely to raise questions and assured her she was fine. She'd then changed the subject to his adorable daughter.

"In the meantime," she continued, brushing, "the Bauers will stay in Billings until Mr. Bauer completes his initial rehab." It had been nearly a week since his heart attack. "He's still expected to make a full recovery," she told him, confirming what Kate had learned days ago, "but they won't come back to the lodge until the end of next week. The new couple will stay for a while to help with the maintenance, but Uncle Matthew wants to know if you can keep the horses until Dave can take care of them himself."

She worked toward the horse's rump, trying to gain a little distance from the man who'd resurrected the deep-seated restiveness she'd almost managed to escape.

"If you want me to go when the new people get here, I will. But if I go to my aunt and uncle's lodge, I'd like to take the horses with me. I can care for them for the Bauers myself as long as I'm here."

If he wants her to go, she'd said.

Curious to know what she wanted, and more than a little

surprised by how much that mattered, he thumbed back the brim of his hat by an inch and narrowed his eyes on her profile. "Why would you want to stay?"

Because I would miss your daughter, she thought, *even though you don't let me spend any more time with her than is necessary. Because I'm drawn to you in ways I can't explain. Because I need to know why you wouldn't kiss me…*

Her last thought had come unbidden. "Because I'd miss cooking with Kate and talking with Wiley," she told him, dismissing it. She really didn't want to know why he hadn't. Neither of her options was favorable. "And because I'd like a chance to see more of your rangeland," she admitted, because she wanted to see beyond where she'd been. All this space, and he'd limited her to so little of it. "I've only ridden out to where the road by the creek ends at the little waterfall."

"Creek End Falls is a mile away." His scowl entered his voice. "Why did you go that far?"

She kept brushing. "Because I could."

He could point out that he'd asked her not to go any farther than the road leading to the highway. But technically, she hadn't. She'd just kept going where that road curved. He said nothing about that, though. It wasn't rebellion he sensed in her, anyway. Not against him. What he sensed in her was more a need for the freedom she seemed to want so badly. Still, he didn't care at all for her being so far out on her own.

"You could get lost…"

"Not following the creek up and back," she countered ever so reasonably.

"…and I've warned you about coyotes and snakes. They can spook a horse. You shouldn't be taking those risks."

"From what I've heard from Kate and your men, life on a ranch like this poses all kinds of risks. Since you take risks every day, why can't I? And please don't tell me it's because I'm your responsibility," she continued before he could say a word, "and that you told my uncle you'd take care of me. Forget who I am for a minute and tell me why I shouldn't do something I'm perfectly capable of doing, and which you wouldn't give a second's thought to doing yourself."

She sent him a level glance. There was no mistaking the challenge in it in the moment before she turned back to her task. There seemed to be more to that challenge, too, than just how far she could ride, but all he considered was that he couldn't let himself forget who she was. She would be far too dangerous if he did.

That was why he'd looked up her and Valdovia on the Internet last night. He'd seen pictures of the huge palace she lived in and images of her royal family; the elderly queen who ruled them all, the Princess Royal and Sophie's father, a prince in his own right. Other than a family photo, the only images of her had been of her reading to children and an official portrait in which she'd been gowned, crowned and sashed.

In every one of them, she'd looked very much the dutiful princess. Yet, in not one of those pictures had he seen any of the sass and spirit he knew she possessed. From the way she so often disappeared behind her facade of calm, he had the feeling she'd been taught to bury that spirit and spontaneity right along with the frustration so evident in her now.

Watching her agitated motions, it was obvious her considerable composure tended to crack around him. He just couldn't help wonder if that was because she trusted him to see her as she truly was, or if he somehow goaded her guard into slipping.

Remembering his attitude toward her when she'd first

arrived, he suspected her composure would have held up if she'd wanted it, too.

That left trust.

Knowing how hard that was for her to come by seemed to put a dent in his own armor.

"Did you tell Wiley where you were going?"

He saw her hesitate. "No."

"From now on, check in with him before you leave and when you get back."

Her shoulders went still. A moment later, they seemed to sag. "Fine."

She didn't want to be reined in. He hated feeling he was doing that to her now. Still, he'd found himself worrying about her. And not only because she was his friend's niece.

"About you taking the horses to your uncle's," he prefaced, not comfortable with that, either. He didn't like the idea of her taking care of the horses alone, or of her going to stay with strangers. He overlooked the fact that until a few days ago, everyone she associated with now had been a stranger to her. "Tell Matt he's welcome to leave them here. We'll talk about you taking them with you if it comes to that.

"Tell me something," he continued, dismissing what felt like possessiveness simply as part of keeping her safe. "Why is working with these horses so important to you? Do you train them or do competitions or something where you're from?"

She'd mentioned that she loved to jump. He could easily see her riding steeplechase or show jumping or whatever the genteel version of rodeo happened to be.

"I'm not good enough to compete." Unlike her oldest sister, Sophie thought. Isabella hadn't made it to the Olympics the way Princess Anne of England had, but she'd been on the Valdovian national team. "All I do is ride them," she said, thinking of how her only two competitions had resulted in headlines comparing her ever-so-unfavorably to her more accomplished sibling. Rather than have her reflect badly on the family again, it had been deemed that equestrian competition was not her forte. "And help groom them if the stable master isn't around."

At home, it wasn't considered proper for her to do what she was doing now. The groomsmen and stable boys had their duties. Duties in which they took great pride. It embarrassed them when she wanted to help. She told Carter that. She told him, too, that her mother had once informed her that a royal taking over a servant's job made the servant feel as if he weren't doing his duties properly, or as if the royal was amusing herself with what to him was his livelihood. There were protocols to maintain. Lines that weren't to be crossed.

"As good as you are, why don't you train? Or teach?"

His matter-of-fact compliment gave her pause. "I'd love to," she told him, surprised he thought her skills anything but ordinary. "I'd especially love to work at my grandmother's riding school for children, but that's Isabella's thing. There isn't enough room for two of us there."

"So start your own."

He made it sound so easy. "I don't have my sister's credentials. The Crown would never approve.

"I'll just enjoy being with them like I always have. When I was young," she mused, "the stables were the first place I'd go when something went wrong. Since that seemed to be every other day," she confided easily, "I learned to love it there. The animals didn't care about protocol. They didn't care if I stood properly. Or if my curtsy wasn't deep enough. Or if I was more of a tomboy, or more of a disappointment than my family wished me to be.

"And they certainly didn't care about my bloodlines, though theirs were analyzed, prized and scrutinized as much as my own." Crossing her right boot in front of her left knee, she knocked the brush against the side of her boot. Horsehair and dirt landed on the planks. "It's rather pathetic, really, to have your bloodlines determine your value."

She went back to her methodical brushing. Only now the agitation was back. That same uncharacteristic note had drained the spirit from her voice.

He couldn't imagine her disappointing anyone. Not with a heart as generous as hers seemed to be. Days ago, he wouldn't have been able to imagine her as a tomboy, either. With her easy grace, the image still didn't come easily, even dressed as she was in denim and baggy fleece.

"Are you talking about horses?" he asked mildly. "Or yourself?"

Her glance darted to his, only to self-consciously slip away.

He wasn't sure what he'd seen in her eyes. Not liking what he suspected, he caught her chin and tipped her face toward his.

Her heredity dictated how she lived her life, no matter her own desires or needs. As much as that bothered him, something about her lineage bothered him even more. "Do you think people care about you only because of your bloodlines?"

The dejection he'd glimpsed lingered there. Even her soft smile couldn't completely hide it.

"I hope not," she murmured, "but that's not something I can ever know for sure. That's why I like being here. On your ranch, with Kate and your men," she qualified, because she knew he saw her differently, "I'm just someone helping out. In their own ways, they treat me just like everyone else. At home, that would never happen."

Beneath his fingers, he could feel the incredible softness of her skin. Yet, he was conscious more of the loneliness in her he would never have suspected she felt. Not just loneliness, he thought, considering what he'd just heard. Isolation.

Sophie's heart bumped against her breastbone. With his eyes narrowed on hers, his touch gentle on her face, her voice fell to little more than a whisper. "This wouldn't, either."

She hadn't moved from his touch. She'd done nothing but look up at him with those liquid brown eyes and make him forget he wasn't supposed to be touching her at all. The way her head moved slightly into his touch made it seem as if she needed that small contact as much as he felt the need for it himself.

"What do you mean?" he asked, brushing his thumb beneath her lower lip. Its fullness beckoned him. The scent of her, warm and faintly provocative drew him closer. "That a man wouldn't want to kiss you?"

Her breath seemed to go shallow. "That I would want him to," she whispered.

The quiet admission had him going still. Conscious of all she'd told him, his voice dropped to a low rumble. "You don't get what you want very often, do you?"

With his eyes narrowed on hers, she gave a small, almost indiscernible shake of her head.

"That's what I thought," he murmured, and cupped her face with both hands.

It's just a kiss, he told himself, lowering his head to hers. Just a kiss to take away that lonely look from her eyes. But that was before he felt the softness of her mouth beneath his and he breathed in her small sigh.

The warmth of her breath filled his lungs.

Her small hands fisted his shirt.

The quick heat darting through him as his tongue touched

hers demanded that he kiss her more deeply, that he pull her taut little body into his arms and know the feel of her small breasts against his chest. She would fit perfectly there. She would fit perfectly everywhere. Yet, even as she swayed closer, the part of his brain that knew he shouldn't be doing this at all, forced his hands to stay where they were. Though he ached to at least explore the sweet, seductive taste of her, he eased back enough to move his lips to one corner of her mouth. Then, to the other.

Sophie's fingers gripped his shirt more tightly. Beneath her fists, she could feel the strong beat of his heart. His mouth looked so hard, yet it felt incredibly soft as it moved lightly along her lower lip.

No man had ever kissed her so gently before.

No man had ever kissed her with a tenderness that threatened to bring the sting of tears to her eyes.

No man had ever left her so shaken by the unfamiliar yearnings inside her when he finally lifted his head and eased her back.

Carter's breathing felt decidedly unsteady. With his body demanding more, his mind telling him he'd done more than he should, his hands drifted from her face. "That wasn't because you're a princess," he told her. "That was just a kiss between friends."

"Hey, Carter. There you are," said a voice from beyond the wide end doors. "Got time to take a call from Ty?" With his back to Wiley, his big frame shielding hers, he let his hands fall. "Sure thing, Wiley," he called. "I'm on my way."

With that, he handed her the brush she'd dropped and headed for the open doors, swearing at himself on the way.

When he'd walked in, he had been dead certain he had everything under control as far as Sophie was concerned. Walking back out, he wondered how in the hell he was supposed to keep his hands to himself when all he really wanted to do was take her to bed.

Still, despite the fact that her taste now coursed through his blood, keeping his hands to himself was exactly what he intended to do.

Chapter Nine

Carter usually slept with his bedroom door open so he could hear Hanna. Since Sophie had arrived, he'd been leaving it almost closed. It just seemed more proper that way. Still, he slept lightly, with one ear attuned, the way he did when he slept in the stables when a mare was due to give birth. He hadn't heard anything specific when he'd wakened a minute ago, even though he'd lain there listening. Instinct had just pulled him from his bed and to his daughter's room, where he found Sophie sitting on the edge of Hanna's bed, stroking his little girl's hair.

Standing in Hanna's doorway in his pajama bottoms, he watched Sophie glance up. Without a sound, she rose from his daughter's bed, a pale apparition in a white nightshirt that covered her arms, but bared her knees. As she carefully pulled the blanket up to Hanna's chin, he could see that her hair was down. The dark length of it flowed like a veil to the middle of her shoulder blades.

He hadn't seen her since he'd left her in the stables. Caution now seemed to radiate from her as she left Hanna and crossed the shadowy space while he backed into the equally dim hall. The nightlight at the end of the hallway allowed shapes to be visible, but colors were only shades of gray. In that pale light, her guarded glance jerked from his bare chest as she moved from the door she hadn't quite closed.

"I think she had a nightmare," she murmured, her voice as quiet as the still, silent house. "When she came into my room, she asked if she could sleep with me."

She looked impossibly young with her hair spilling behind her back, the delicate line of her collarbone exposed by her nightshirt. Mostly, she looked like temptation.

Pulling his focus back to her face, he pointedly kept it there. He never should have kissed her. Now that he knew the taste of her... "Why didn't you get me?" he asked, ruthlessly slicing off the thought.

"I didn't want to disturb you," she said. "As late as it was when you got in, I knew you had to be exhausted." She glanced toward Hanna's room, motioned him with her a few more steps down the hall so they couldn't be overheard. "After I told her I wouldn't leave until she went back to sleep, she seemed okay with going back to her own bed.

"I'm sure she would have gone to you," she hurried to add, as if she knew he didn't like the idea of his daughter turning to her instead of him. "But she was asleep when you returned. She probably didn't know you were back."

With his door nearly closed, Hanna would have known he was there, Carter thought. But more important just then was his need to know what had disturbed his daughter. "Why do you think she had a nightmare?"

"Because of what she told me," Sophie whispered. "She

wasn't crying when she first came in, but she was teary and hugging her doll. She said she kept running but couldn't find anyone. Then she said she was waiting in a room, but no one ever came for her."

He couldn't have been asleep for more than an hour, Sophie thought, studying the chiseled angles of his face. She'd heard him come in. Heard his shower go on. As close as they stood to keep their quieted voices from carrying, every breath she took brought the scents of soap and warm male.

Even in the dim light she could see that he'd shaved. By morning, he'd need to shave again, but now, the hard line of his jaw looked as smooth as marble. So did the rest of his hard, honed body as her glance strayed over the sculpted lines of his powerful arms and shoulders, his broad, bare chest and the ripple of abs above the low drawstring waist of dark, soft-looking flannel.

His nearness disturbed her as much as the memory of how soft his mouth had been on hers. But now his mouth thinned, tightening his jaw and taunting her with an entirely different sort of tension.

"She's had that dream before," he muttered. He pushed his fingers through his hair, his biceps looking huge in the moments before his hand fell. "Or ones similar to it. Just not for the last month or so."

Part of her wanted to take a step back, to put a little space between her and all that raw, tense muscle. The part of her that needed to offer what his child could not kept her right where she was.

A kiss between friends.

That's all it had been, because that was all they could be.

"Maybe the dream returned because you've been gone so much the past week. I'm not a psychologist," she prefaced, as disappointed as she was grateful to know how he regarded her, "but I know she worries about you not coming back. Maybe she was dreaming—" *that you abandoned her,* she thought "—that she'd been left alone," she concluded, because it sounded less worrisome that way.

He looked worried, anyway. That concern had etched itself as deeply as the fatigue in his shadowed face. There was something else, there, too, something that looked a little dangerous and a lot protective.

"Did she say anything else?"

Sophie shook her head. "Just that she was scared to be alone. Talk to her about her dream in the morning, Carter. That might help both of you. Especially if you explain why you have to be so late right now."

"I have explained."

"You might want to do it again. She's little," she quietly reminded him. "A day is forever to her. Maybe she needs for you to remind her every morning for a while that this is temporary, and reassure her that you'll come back whenever you leave. You have to know that couldn't hurt."

He eyed her evenly. "What I know," he said, a razor-thin edge on the low tones of his voice, "is that she needs a mother, and that hers is probably the reason she's afraid I'll walk out on her, too."

Frustration fairly leaked from his pores as he lifted his hand, clamped it over the still-sore muscle in his shoulder.

"I'm not totally sure what happened while she was with Tiffany," he said tightly. "I don't think she ever left Hanna alone, but I got the feeling from the gal who dropped her off that Tiff left her with people Hanna didn't know for two or three days at a time."

Which, Sophie realized, had to be why he hadn't wanted

to leave Hanna with her, and why he wouldn't leave her overnight with Truly. She knew from Kate that the veterinarian's wife had offered a couple of times now to keep her the rest of the week.

"Did you see her while she was living with her mother?"

His voice was a sleep-roughed murmur as he told her he'd seen her as often as he could. His wife had moved to Denver, so he'd flown there every other week to see his little girl. The frustration Sophie had felt in him moments ago seemed to succumb to weariness as he then mentioned that Hanna had barely been three when Tiffany had taken her away, and that his child had clung to him like a burr whenever it had been time for him to go.

There had been pain in those partings. For Carter and for his daughter. There was no doubt of that in Sophie's mind as he drew a deep breath, then shook his head as if to shake off the unwelcome memory.

"It's not like Hanna can't count on me," he insisted.

No, Sophie thought. It's not like that at all.

"What about her mother? Has she seen her since she sent her back?"

"She didn't want visitation. She signed away all her rights after she moved to New York. I have sole custody."

Sophie opened her mouth. Closed it again. Questions piled up like cars in a train wreck as she tried to imagine what could make a woman walk away so completely from her husband and child. The husband part wasn't so difficult, she conceded, considering what she knew of some men. But leaving a child a woman had birthed and nurtured for over four years took more imagination than she apparently had.

She couldn't help wondering, either, what had drawn him

to the woman he'd cared for enough to marry, and what had gone so wrong in the aftermath.

He'd mentioned Denver and New York. New York, she knew, was huge. "Was Tiffany from a big city?"

The cynicism in his quiet laugh made it a snort. "She grew up right here. She was the daughter of a ranch hand who'd worked for my father."

"So you actually had a lot in common."

"I thought we did. But you know how that goes," he reminded her. "I thought we wanted the same things," he said, echoing what she'd told him about the last man she'd trusted. "Turns out that we didn't."

That sort of mutual disappointment was a lousy bond to share.

"What did you want?" she asked, needing to know that, too.

It was impossible to know exactly what he was looking for as he quietly searched her features. The assurance that she did understand, perhaps. Or, maybe, that he could trust her as she had trusted him with what he was about to say. Whatever it was, he seemed to find it in the long moments before he let the door to that part of his past crack open enough to let her glimpse inside.

"A home. A family." He shrugged. "To continue my father's legacy," he said, though the lift of his massive shoulders had done nothing to dismiss how important that had been to him. "I knew when I married her that her life hadn't been easy. Her mom took off when she was a kid and her dad couldn't hang on to a job more than a year or two at a time. They lived pretty much all over the state.

"She said she wanted roots." His voice dropped even lower as, still facing her, he leaned one shoulder against the wall. "And I guess I was feeling a need to protect my own roots after Dad died. I know I was," he admitted, letting the opening crack wider. "For the first couple of months after he passed away, she was always coming up here to see if there was anything she could do for me. One thing led to another," he said, deliberately omitting what those things were, "and we got married."

With her arms loosely crossed over her cotton nightshirt, she rested her shoulder against the wall, too. "How long was it before you realized there were problems?"

He gave his head a slow shake. "I can't say for sure. I knew she'd never had much of her own, but once she had a taste of a few nice things, she kept wanting more. She had ideas about the kind of home she wanted from magazines she'd collected," he told her, "so she started changing things around here pretty much as soon as she moved in. Since she was my wife and this was her home, too, I figured she could do what she wanted as long as she left my den alone.

"I didn't much care for some of her choices," he allowed, explaining without saying so why upscale urban chic competed with rustic in parts of the house. "But it wasn't long before changing the things around her wasn't enough. She started to try to change me, and the way we lived."

And she would cry and pout when he refused to cooperate, he remembered. Then, she'd go on streaks where she'd cook his favorite meals or greet him at the door wearing boots, a cowgirl hat and not much more to see if those means could coax him to her way of thinking.

He didn't mention the latter. Or that he'd finally realized about the time she got pregnant with Hanna, that the only time Tiffany did things for him was when she wanted something—which had eventually made him wonder if she'd ever really cared about him at all, or if he'd always just been a means to an end.

"Long story short," he muttered, burying details he didn't want to remember anyway, "she decided she hated everything about ranching and wanted to live in a city. I told her I couldn't leave here." He'd tried to explain why, but she hadn't cared. He'd reminded her that this life was part of what she married. Her response was that he wasn't being sensitive to her needs. "She said if I wouldn't come with her, she'd go without me. So…she did.

"Eighteen months later, she moved east. In the letter she sent with Hanna, she said she'd grown past what she'd had to live with in Montana and that she wanted no reminders of a life she'd rather forget."

That last reminder had been her daughter.

The acknowledgment of that inescapable fact hung between them in the sudden quiet.

To Sophie, it seemed there could be no more total rejection of a man than to also reject his child. From what Carter had just said, though, the woman sounded very much like a product of a totally dysfunctional childhood. Tiffany had abandoned her daughter just as her mother had abandoned her. Considering her vagabond life with her ranch hand father, she might well have moved on from any man who raised cattle for a living.

That didn't excuse what she'd done. It just explained it.

The furnace kicked on, the first rush of cool air ahead of warm bumping the loose grate in the dining room. In the still hallway, she saw Carter's eyes narrow on hers.

"What?" he asked, as if he could feel her pondering.

"Please tell me I'm not that easy to read."

"Only if you want me to lie to you."

The faintest of smiles formed on her lips. "The honesty thing."

"Yeah," he murmured. "That." She had those twin lines between her eyebrows. They were a dead giveaway that she had a question. "So...?"

"I just wondered if you'd loved her."

He hesitated. Not because of the question, but because, with her, he felt no risk answering it.

"I don't know," he admitted, because he didn't quite know how the emotion was supposed to feel. "As much as anything, I cared about her for being around after Dad died, and for the possibilities life with her seemed to promise.

"Those possibilities were already dead when she left," he admitted, his deep voice still hushed. "And so were whatever feelings I'd had for her. By the time we got through all the legal hassles, all I felt was relief that I didn't have to deal with her anymore."

That relief had been huge, but so had been the resentment that had scarred over the regret and disappointment.

It seemed he didn't have to admit that for Sophie to understand how thick those protective scars were.

"Do you think you'll ever marry again?"

Had anyone else asked the question, he'd have muttered something about hell freezing over. As honest as he'd pressed her to be with him, as much as he couldn't believe he'd already told her, she didn't deserve that knee-jerk defensiveness.

"The only reason I'd want a wife is to have a mother for my daughter and a couple of sons to carry on the ranch. As timid as Hanna is around the animals, I can't imagine her wanting to work this place. After I'm gone, there's no one to care about it."

"So you'd marry out of duty to the land. I'm not being critical," she insisted, not sure if it was marriage or her conclusion that drew his frown. "My family has been marrying to keep land and property in the family for centuries. Someday, I'll marry some duke or prince who will be marrying me out of a sense of duty, too."

She gave a little sigh. "It's just that when a person marries, it seems that the rough patches would be easier to weather if love was involved. Duty has always impressed me as a rather depressing reason for two adults to promise to spend the rest of their lives together."

Despite her small, resigned smile, nothing about his expression changed. "That's why you'll marry?" he asked. "Out of a sense of obligation?"

"I'm not obligated to marry," she said quietly. "But I will. I want children, too, so I'll marry someone looking to preserve his royal bloodlines. At least that way, I'll know why he's married me," she pointed out, clearly not caring to suffer any fantasies about being wanted for herself. "It's rather hard to feel betrayed when one has no illusions to begin with."

That afternoon in the stables, Carter had bumped squarely into the uncertainty her lineage placed on her when it came to relationships. Coming upon it again, he could see what he'd missed before. It was as if having been betrayed by less pedigreed men, she'd chosen to regard herself as a commodity, as someone whose only value existed because she was a means of preserving a heritage.

He understood all about bloodlines when it came to producing healthy cattle, and preserving the pedigrees of horseflesh. But he flat didn't care for the idea of her thinking of herself as breeding stock.

He especially didn't care for the idea of her with some other man.

Not caring to consider why that was, needing to block the forbidden direction his thoughts wanted to go, he focused on the utter practicality of her approach. While the cynic in him could appreciate it, he suspected she wasn't nearly as settled with the idea as she sounded. He couldn't help feeling, either, that she was shortchanging herself big time with what she had to offer a man.

"Will you be happy living like that?"

She shrugged. "I know people who aren't completely miserable in those marriages," she admitted, making it sound as if avoiding abject misery qualified as success. "My parents' separate lives actually seem to suit them fairly well."

"I didn't ask about your parents." Though what she'd just said spoke volumes about her expectations in a relationship. "I asked if you'd be happy."

In the near darkness, her smile looked faintly bittersweet.

"I'll have to be. You, on the other hand," she said softly, "only have to let go of the wall I suspect you've built around your heart and you'll find everything you want."

Lifting her hand, she touched her palm to his cheek. "If I could, I'd gladly trade places with you, Carter McLeod. Since I can't, I'll just try to be more like you. I'll give my heart to things I care about the way you care about your daughter and this ranch. Then, I'll just push myself so hard taking care of them that I won't have time to think about what I'm missing."

Carter wasn't sure what got to him more just then, the somber look in her eyes as they held his, or that she would chose to emulate him at all. He had to be the poorest role model on the planet for a princess.

He might have told her that, too, had he not been struggling with the urge to catch her hand and pull her closer—and fighting the odd sense of loss he felt when her hand slid away.

"You're tired," she told him, mercifully stepping beyond his reach. "Don't worry about Hanna right now," she added because his concern for his daughter was what had brought them to be standing there. "You need sleep." She turned to her room, glanced back once more. "Rest well."

Carter would have sworn rest would be impossible when he rolled back into his bed, trying his best to ignore the aches that had come from pushing his body as if it were ten years younger and the restless needs and aches aroused by the woman in her bed two doors down his hall. There were other needs she aroused, too, needs for the closeness and caring he'd been reminded of as they'd talked in the hall. He just didn't have time to deny them before his body succumbed to its demand for sleep.

The woman was off-limits.

Over the next few days, the phrase became Carter's mantra. He wasn't accustomed to repeating himself, but there were other things he wasn't accustomed to either. Telling a woman she was a friend being one of them. Not that he didn't know females he'd consider friends if he had to label them. Yet, he'd never been even remotely interested in exposing so much of himself to any one of them the way he had with Sophie, not even when they'd hinted, prodded or outright asked about his ex and his plans for the future.

There were things about Sophie, though, that would never allow him to think of her simply as a friend. The effects of her smile, her voice and the remembered taste of her most immediately coming to mind. She was far from an ideal candidate for a nice, uncomplicated physical relationship. But that didn't mean he couldn't ask for more of her insights where his daughter was concerned. Or that he couldn't appreciate that she started his coffee brewing for him every morning before she departed for the cookhouse, and how he'd find an extra slice of whatever pie or cobbler she and Kate had baked waiting on the island for him at the end of another long day. If Hanna was still up, she would be there, too, to tell him she helped bake it.

He found it nice to have that pie while they talked because he liked how Sophie seemed truly interested in what he had to say. But, after he'd tuck Hanna in or go kiss her good-night, he couldn't help thinking how much nicer it would be to end the evening with Sophie in his arms instead of closed in her room when he headed into his own.

He allowed himself to look forward to being with her. There was no reason not to. After all, as he kept reminding himself, she would be leaving soon. Just not as soon as he'd thought. The couple Sophie's aunt had told her about had arrived, but when Sophie had told him that, he'd felt as unenthused about the news as she'd looked.

It had surprised him to realize that he wasn't ready yet for her to go. He'd dismissed any significance to the silent admission, however, and earned her quietly relieved smile by telling her it didn't make sense for her to leave right now. She had her routine there and the other people needed time to settle in. She might as well stay until the Bauers returned. What he didn't say was that he had no idea who the other people were or how comfortable she'd be with them. At least he knew she'd like Jenny and Dave.

Aside from that bit of protectiveness, they'd finished up branding last week and chores on the ranch had turned to the spring work of fence repair, seeding, spraying and such. Now that he had some time, he'd show her something he thought she might like to see before she had to leave.

He hadn't told her what that something was. He'd just asked her to meet him in the workshop after she finished up at the cookhouse and Kate left with Hanna.

He'd always been his own man, made his own decisions, his own choices. Obligation and duty might well have led him on the path he'd chosen, but in the end, his choices had been his and his alone. He couldn't imagine living life as she did, hemmed in by what she could say and do, whom she could associate with, and accountable to nearly everyone. He couldn't give her the freedom she craved, but he could share the sense of it with her.

She'd said she wanted to see more of his land. Since he had to cross a fair section of it tomorrow, he might as well show it to her.

"You're taking me out on the range?"

Sophie spoke over the clatter of the wide-toothed rake and an axe Carter dropped onto the metal bed of the truck he'd backed through the wide workshop door. A chainsaw from a long, tool-strewn workbench followed. That was joined by a coil of rope he took from atop several others piled beside a huge spool of thick-linked chain. A pair of green rubber waders similar to what she'd seen her father wear fly-fishing went in next.

"I have a chore to tend," Carter replied, preferring to focus on what needed to be done, rather than what had prompted his invitation. The two-birds-with-one-stone theory sat better with him than acknowledging the soft spot he'd developed toward his charge. He felt bad for the woman, was all.

"You said you wanted to see more of the land," he reminded her, searching out the cooler he'd packed for himself from the one the women had prepared the men for lunch. He'd tossed in an extra sandwich for her. "Since I'm heading about ten miles out, I figured you might like to come along."

As delighted as Sophie was at the prospect, she dubiously eyed what he'd gathered. "What sort of a chore?"

"Clearing a stream. When I was flying over yesterday, I noticed that a section of Bitterbrush Creek is dammed up."

She knew he'd flown over his land yesterday. She'd been talking with Wiley outside the pasture the horses grazed in when a small, white plane had flown overhead. Wiley had squinted up, said that the boss must be checking herds, then ambled back to his chores. That evening, when she'd asked Carter how often he checked his cattle that way, he told her he did it once a week at least. It was the easiest way to track the herds and check for strays. Especially in winter after a storm.

She liked listening to him at the end of the day. Partly because she found it fascinating. Mostly because when he talked, it seemed to remove the fine tension that tended to slip into their silences.

He hadn't touched her since he'd left her yearning for what she'd so briefly felt in the stables days ago. He hadn't even responded to her when she'd touched him that same night in the hall. Where conversation had become easy between them, just being with him sometimes was not.

Something inside her ached for the connection she'd felt when he'd kissed her; the simple need to be touched, to be held. But he hadn't held her. He'd just given her a taste of what she hadn't known existed, and walked away.

She'd give anything to be in his arms. Even for a little while. "Don't you want to go?"

"Yes! Of course," she amended, a little less emphatically.

"Then, what's the matter?"

As easy as it had become to speak her mind with him, there were some things she simply couldn't bring herself to say.

Keeping her mouth shut, she shook her head.

"Come on, then," he said and opened the passenger door of the truck so she could climb in.

Her rides along the little creek below the road had been beautiful. The creek itself was about as wide as her arm-spread and about that far from the deer path she followed. One side was heavy with trees and low brush. The other lay wide and flat until it bumped into bald hills a half day's ride away.

She'd seen wild flowers and rabbits. Breathed in air fresh with scents of loamy earth and bushes she didn't recognize. But she hadn't been prepared for the vistas that opened up as he drove past the fields he would start tilling tomorrow to plant alfalfa for hay for winter feed, or those beyond the ridge line that overlooked an enormous valley.

That untouched rangeland seemed to stretch forever.

Below them, copses of aspen and pine dotted the spring-green scrub grass covering the valley floor. Wildflowers brushed swaths of yellow, purple and orange like long spills of paint. A wide stream that looked more like a river to her cut through it all in a glittering gray ribbon. On either side of it roamed hundreds of rust-colored cattle. In the distance, a range of jagged snowcapped mountains stood sentinel over it all.

"Wow." Eloquent, Sophie was not. But that was her gut reaction to the sheer majesty of the place Carter called home. It was no wonder he could never leave this place.

She heard him chuckle, the rich, deep sound pulling her

glance across the truck's wide bench seat. The view had nearly taken her breath away. The sight of him smiling at her with
pure pleasure in his eyes...did.

His glance strayed to the curve of her mouth. "Yeah," he
murmured, and put the truck into gear to head them down the
other side of the ridge.

It took another half an hour to drive over the rutted cow
path they followed to get to their destination.

The narrow stream flowing through the smaller valley had
been blocked by a tree that had fallen from the stands of cot-
tonwoods growing along it. With the snowmelt getting
heavier as the weather warmed, the rushing water had piled
up loose vegetation from farther upstream behind all those
leafy branches and limbs, raising the water to its banks behind
it and cutting the flow on the other side by half.

Sophie asked if she could help.

Carter hesitated. Beneath the brim of his Stetson, he looked
as if he wasn't sure he wanted her getting that close to the
equipment he'd need to cut the tree up and haul it out.

"I'm storing up experiences, Carter," she coaxed, sensing
his protectiveness. There was something comforting about his
brand of it. It wasn't oppressive. It didn't seek to control, mold
or dictate so much as to...care for.

She'd never known that kind of protectiveness existed. He
couldn't begin to know how unfair it was of him to let her know
it did. Once she left there, she might well never feel it again.

Like she might never feel the quick, unfamiliar yearnings
she'd experienced when he'd kissed her.

"Storing up experiences, huh?"

"Precisely."

From the way he stood with his hands on his hips, his expression inscrutable, she couldn't tell if he was pondering her

need to soak up everything she could about this raw, rugged and peaceful place, or if he was coming up with something she could do that didn't involve the chain saw or the axe.

She still had no idea what he'd been thinking when he tossed her a pair of leather work gloves two sizes too big and asked her to get the rope from the back of the truck.

It took three hours of cutting, sawing, hauling, chopping and hauling some more before the chore was done. By the time it was, she could see why he bought analgesic cream and anti-inflammatories in the giant, economy size. They were also both a little wet. But when he asked if she'd like to see the old homestead, the place his great-grandfather had originally built, on the way back, all thoughts of wet boots, damp jeans and scratches disappeared with her instant smile.

Carter wasn't sure why he wanted to show her the dilapidated old place with its moss-covered walls and the roof that had caved in from too many winters of heavy snow. It just seemed important to him that she know just how humble his roots were. Or, maybe, what he was doing was reminding himself of that because what he really wanted to do was pull the clip from her hair, cover her smile with his mouth and lay her on the carpet of leaves and moss by that quietly rushing stream. He'd never met a woman who could so easily delight in something as simple as a wildflower.

They never made it to the homestead, though. They were on the bladed road used to haul hay out to cattle in winter when he caught a glimpse of a rust-colored calf by a sage bush from the corner of his eye.

The pleasure he took in Sophie's smile when she spotted it, too, didn't last long, though. Except for having done battle with a bramble thicket, the calf seemed okay, but its mama wasn't around anywhere. A calf alone was never a good sign—which was why finding its mother took precedence over reminding himself that what he and Sophie were sharing had nowhere to go.

Chapter Ten

Carter had no idea what Sophie was thinking when he dropped her off at the house for her to meet Hanna returning with Kate at eight that evening. With an orphaned calf that needed feeding, its cuts swabbed and an antibiotic to ward off infection, he headed with the animal for the barn. She hadn't said much on the ride back. Busy reminding himself of how alien his world was to her, and how refined and civilized her own had to be, he hadn't said much, either.

They'd finally found the calf's mother, dead, a mile away at the bottom of a shallow ravine. His terse oath when he'd spotted it had held regret for the loss, but in the time it had taken for him to push Sophie back from the sorry sight, his concern had moved to the calf that had just lost its food supply. One thing he could do nothing about. The other he could. So that was where he'd focused. There, and on the woman who sometimes made it hard to remember that she wasn't part of his reality.

She was using her temporary asylum to store up experiences. She'd said as much that afternoon. This was fantasy to her; an escape she could look back on from the ivory tower he'd started to forget she lived in. For his own sake as much as hers, he probably shouldn't have taken her with him that day at all.

That conclusion nagged like a festering splinter the whole time he tended the calf. It continued to nag at him all the way back to the house.

Carter had returned over half an hour ago.

Sophie finished drying her hair in front of the steam-circled bathroom mirror, still troubled by the distance she'd sensed in him in the brief moments they'd spoken in the kitchen. When she'd asked about the calf, he'd assured her that it was doing fine, then said he was going to tuck Hanna in and head for the shower. She understood that Hanna didn't need to hear anything that might bring on a nightmare, but from the way he'd all but dismissed her own presence, it was as if she'd had no part in all that had happened that day.

She had waited for him to return before she'd showered off the creek water that had made her denims stick to her skin and the musky smell of the calf she'd helped secure in the back of the truck. She hadn't wanted to miss him. There were questions she wanted to ask and something she needed to say, but all that would apparently have to wait until morning.

With her hair finally dry and tucked behind her ears, she tightened the belt of her white spa robe and turned the knob on the door. The door of his bedroom slanted open partway when she stepped into the light of the hall. As if he'd been listening for her, it opened the rest of the way before she could take more than a step toward her room.

He'd just finished showering, too. Pulling on a fresh chambray shirt over a clean pair of worn jeans, he walked toward her, barefoot. His dark hair was still damp.

"I wanted to catch you before you went to bed," he said, his deep voice low as he moved past her to Hanna's door.

Carter peeked inside. Finding his daughter sleeping, he pulled the door to so they wouldn't disturb her. "To make sure you're all right," he explained, because he needed to know. Part of him felt defensive because one of the tougher aspects of his life had wrecked his attempt at chivalry. Another part, the concerned part, felt bad for whatever he'd left her dealing with. "I know we had a bawling calf in the back so it was hard to talk, but you seemed pretty quiet coming back here."

His guarded eyes scanned her face, moved a little more slowly over the beautiful hair spilling straight and glossy behind her shoulders. Her bathrobe was even more modest than the nightgown he'd seen her in last week. White terry-cloth covered her from neck to ankle. Still, she seemed conscious of having been caught in it as she tucked one lapel a little more securely beneath the other.

"I was just thinking about the day," she told him, as he pulled his glance from between her breasts. "And about this place."

He could only imagine what had been going through her mind. The day had not turned out at all the way he'd intended. All he'd wanted to do was to give her something *she'd* wanted by showing her more of his land. The more ruthless aspects of Mother Nature hadn't been on his agenda at all.

He watched her study him, her expression calm and considering.

That same thoughtfulness entered her tone.

"Life is very real here, isn't it?"

Her soft words were far more statement than question.

They also proved to him all over again that she never did see things quite the way he would have expected. She could easily have seen his ruggedly beautiful land as he'd first described it to her; as merciless, ruthless, unfair. Yet what she'd seen was its simplicity, and how very basic it was.

He couldn't help but wonder if that was because her own world held such pretension.

"Yeah, well," he muttered, wondering what they'd think of her in that world now, "you got a better taste of it than I'd intended." The dark slashes of his eyebrows drew together as he took a step toward her. Taking her by the chin, he tipped her head to one side. "You're all scratched up." A trio of scrapes ran from beneath her ear toward the flat neckline of her robe. Results of wresting the tree limbs she'd hauled for him, no doubt.

Another scratch bisected them, ending near the hollow of her throat.

"You need ointment on these," he said, as conscious of her heart pulsing there as he was of the light, fresh scents of her from her shower.

The feel of his hand on her face had Sophie's voice going even quieter.

"I don't have any."

"I do. Come on."

His fingers slid away even as he turned in the direction he'd come. Moving farther from Hanna's room, Sophie stopped short of his bedroom door.

A king-sized bed with a massive dark wood headboard dominated the purely masculine space. Its navy sheets and heavy burgundy comforter were tossed back in the tangle he'd left them in when his feet had hit the floor early that morning. Somewhere beyond the heavy, carved dresser, she could hear the sound of a cabinet close.

Carter emerged from his bathroom, glancing to where she stood a few feet outside his doorway. The overhead light in the hall touched the hints of gold in her shining brown hair. In the soft light from the brass lamps on his nightstands he noticed two little lines forming between the delicate arches of her eyebrows.

"Was today typical for you?" she asked.

"As typical as any day ever is around here," he said, thinking of the work, discounting the pleasure he'd taken in much of it being with her. Uncapping the antibacterial ointment, he squeezed a bead onto his index finger and handed the tube and cap to her. "Tilt your head."

Snagging back her hair, she tipped her head to her left.

"So you never really know what you'll be doing?" she asked.

With the tip of his finger, he followed the shorter abrasion from behind her ear to where it ended on its own at the side of her neck. "I know what I plan to do," he told her, his voice low, his touch as gentle as he could make it since he knew his hands were rough. "I just don't always know what's going to get thrown in on top of everything else."

The second scratch started higher and farther back. Nudging aside a lock she hadn't caught, he let his fingers slip into her hair to keep it from getting stuck in the salve. The dark strands felt like warm satin against his skin as he traced the scrape through the baby-fine hairs near her nape.

With her head to one side, the long line of her neck exposed, he felt his touch slow. He wasn't doing anything but tending scratches, yet her nearness had his body feeling tight enough to snap bones.

The quiet tones of her voice drifted toward him.

"I'm sorry we didn't get to the homestead."

It was just as well, he thought. Being alone with her out

there in all that shade and sweet grass might well have had him doing what he ached to do right now.

Just one taste of her skin, he thought. Just one kiss. "Just wasn't meant to be," he muttered.

Sophie wasn't sure why that disappointed her so.

"I'm still grateful for today, Carter. Maybe not the parts that weren't so easy," she qualified as she turned. Her hair tumbled over his hand, covering it as she lifted her head to look up at him. "But thank you for sharing it with me."

Her mouth curved then, her smile gentle, her pretty brown eyes holding her gratitude for a day that he wouldn't have regarded as extraordinary at all, except for her presence.

"Hey," he said, feeling a quick and sudden need for perspective. "Anything for a princess."

The smile faded. "Would you please forget that?" she asked, a plea replacing thanks. "Would you please just think of me the way everyone else around here does?"

"I make a point of not doing that."

"Why?"

The muscles in his jaw tightened as his glance pointedly slipped to her mouth. "Because of what will happen if I do," he said, and looked back up.

Sophie felt her heart bump her ribs. Emboldened by the heat in his eyes, praying that he not let her go, she murmured, "What's that?"

"Sophie…"

"What?" she asked, wanting to know just once what would happen if he thought of her only as the woman she was inside. Not as royalty. Not as his charge. Not as the niece of his friend. "Just for a minute, Carter. Just for one minute, forget everything you know about me."

"One minute," he repeated flatly.

"Just one."

That, he could do.

Taking sixty seconds over nothing, allowing himself no further thought than that, he slipped his fingers more securely over the back of her head and tipped her face to his. He'd been dying to do this all day.

At the first brush of his lips to hers, he heard her quiet intake of breath. At the next, she sighed and touched her fingertips to his chest. Opening her to him, he swallowed his own moan at the quick heat spiking through him and gathered her in his arms.

Sophie sagged toward him as her hands flattened against his shirt. Beneath the soft chambray, she could feel the hard beat of his heart, the heavy muscles protecting it. Even with his tongue doing strange, enticing things to her nervous system, in the back of her mind lived the knowledge that his heart was what she wanted.

The realization drew her closer as his hand slipped down her back. The feel of his strong arms surrounding her was more incredible than she could have imagined. This was what she'd wanted, what she'd ached for. This was more than a kiss between friends. More than just a reminder of the quick heat she'd felt when he'd kissed her before. What he made her feel as his hand slipped toward her tailbone and he pressed her to him was his own need. She heard it in his low groan. And that made denying her own need impossible.

Wanting him closer still, she started to curve her arms around his neck. Before she could, he caught her hands by the wrists.

His breathing seemed a little ragged when his kiss drifted to the corner of her mouth. "I think we're coming up on that minute."

The faint vibration of his lips against her skin created new sensations of their own.

Her words came as a whisper as he brushed that kiss to the other side. "How much longer do we have?"

"I wasn't counting," he murmured, bracing himself to let her go, hating the thought. "How much longer do you want?"

Sophie brushed the corner of his mouth as he had hers. She really wasn't terribly experienced at this. She wanted him to teach her, to show her all the things she knew were missing in her life, but right now, she just wanted him to teach her how to make love. He'd already allowed her to experience so much she would never have known without him. By keeping her identity secret from everyone else, he'd made it possible for her to experience life as she would never had known it. With him, she felt free in ways she never had before, and feared she might never again. But more than anything, she feared she'd never know what it was to want a man as badly as he seemed to want her just then.

He couldn't seem to let her go. He was struggling with it, she could tell. But his mouth still hovered over hers.

"Are we talking in terms of minutes?" she asked, her heart hammering. "Or hours?"

Tension curled through him, ruthlessly controlled but unmistakable in its grasp. He craved her. He had no idea how he could want someone so badly when he barely knew the feel of her at all, but one taste of her was all it had taken. Like some illicit drug, he'd been hooked.

Minutes ago, he'd tried not to let himself imagine the feel of her beautiful hair in his hands, but he now knew the amazing texture of it. He'd tried not to imagine the shape of her beneath her robe, but even the feel of her body through all that terrycloth had been enough to turn his blood to steam.

He would have to be made of steel to deny the need in the vulnerable depths of her eyes. Superman he was not. He would have had to be made of rock to deny his own.

"Your call."

Sophie couldn't bear for him to let her go. From out of nowhere came *forever,* but all she whispered to him was, "Until morning."

Wanting her as badly as his next breath, Carter cupped her face in his hands and covered her mouth with his. Within seconds, he was moving them into his room. Blindly easing closed the door as their mouths clung, he pulled her back into his arms.

She'd said she wanted him to forget who she was. But that was impossible. She was the woman who made getting up in the morning a little easier because he knew he'd see her smile that day. She was the woman who had no more of an agenda with him than he did with her. She managed to challenge him without provoking and concede without giving in. He'd never known anyone like her. And when he discovered she wore nothing under her robe but a tiny pair of champagne lace, French-cut underpants, she was the woman who never failed to amaze him with what unexpected and tantalizing detail about her he might discover next.

Sophie's knees threatened to buckle at the feel of his hands on the bare skin of her waist. They did give just a little when she felt them drift up to cup her breasts. Pulling her with him, he sank to the edge of the bed so she could brace her hands on his shoulders in the long moments before he eased the robe onto the floor and her onto his tangled sheets.

She reached for him, feeling self-conscious being so exposed. But he wouldn't let her hide herself. "You're beautiful. You are," he insisted, and made her believe she was as he skimmed his hands over her body, drugging her with the heat of his mouth, the gentleness in his touch.

The creak of a board settling came from somewhere in the house. Beyond its protective walls, a coyote called to its pack. The unfamiliar, eerie sound had awakened Sophie more than once, but each time she'd reminded herself that Carter was there. And that she was safe.

Now, the distant sound barely registered, though that un-questioned sense of safety remained.

Needing to know the feel of him, she slipped her hands beneath his shirt, urging him to pull it off as she ran her hands over the breadth of his wide shoulders. The fabric landed on the floor, allowing her to explore the feel of his muscular arms and back, and the rippled muscles of his abdomen. She did what he had done, trailing kisses after caresses until she reached the waistband of his denims. Something feral swept his carved features when she looked up at him then, and he finally dealt with his jeans and jockeys and her scrap of lace. They'd all landed atop her robe when she heard the nightstand drawer open and he took care to protect her in the moments before she felt his massive thighs brush hers.

She loved this man. The realization should have shaken her. And it might have, had the knowledge not felt so amazingly right when she gripped his arms and rose to meet his kiss once more.

Carter wanted to go slow. From what he understood of her past, it had been a long time for her. Years, he suspected, since the louse who'd betrayed her with the pictures. That was why he'd made himself take his time with her. That, and the need he felt to know every inch of her long, lithe body. As much time as he could, anyway, with the needs of his body clawing at him. But now, his control hung by a thread as he settled himself between her thighs, cradling her to him as her arms wound around his neck.

Capturing her mouth with his, aching for her, he pressed forward.

Her quick intake of breath stopped him cold.

"Please, don't stop," she begged. "It's only supposed to hurt a little."

He could have sworn his heart quit beating. Supposed to? As in, she didn't know?

"Sophie." Her name was a groan on his lips. "I thought…"

"Please, Carter," she whispered. "I want it to be you."

He was her first lover.

The hunger coursing through his veins made the thought nearly impossible to comprehend. But even as her small, soft hands urged him closer and the demands of his body eased him into her warmth, he felt possession join the protectiveness he already felt for her.

In the blue haze that enveloped his brain as she began to move with him, he didn't bother to wonder at the need that had crept in there, too. His only thoughts were of the woman giving herself to him so completely—before the heat they created together vaporized his ability to think at all.

Sophie had left Carter's bed a little before five in the morning. He'd still been asleep when she'd slipped from beneath his arm, but she'd known he'd wake soon. So would Hanna, and she didn't want the child to see her coming from her daddy's room. She knew Carter wouldn't want that, either.

A whole host of insecurities had accompanied her as the newness of her own feelings battled uneasy uncertainty about his. But mostly she felt hope. And anticipation. And a little doubt. But hope fought back.

Her little emotional skirmish still raged as she dressed, then started his morning coffee the way she had all week. She'd all but begged him to make love to her the first time. When they'd wakened in each others arms a couple of hours later, the initiative had been all his. Still, she had no idea what he would think of the direction their relationship had taken.

She now knew he hadn't realized until last night that she'd never been with a man before. But, then, she'd never made it clear that she hadn't. Except for Paolo. She'd admitted ending that relationship because getting her into his bed was all the man had wanted. Carter hadn't seemed put off by her inexperience, though. He'd just held her for a long time after their breathing had quieted.

She now knew, too, that being in love felt about as secure as riding a see-saw without holding on. No sooner had she sensed him entering the room than her uncertainties seemed to knot in her chest.

A couple of frantic heartbeats later, his hand slipped across her shoulder.

"Mornin'," he murmured, and bent to nuzzle the sensitive spot behind her ear.

"Good morning," she whispered back, more relieved than he could possibly imagine to have him touching her again.

She turned into his arms. Within seconds, he swept a glance across her face, drew her to him and kissed her with enough heat to alter her heart rate and his breathing before he lifted his head.

"Are you okay?" he asked, concern in his hooded gray eyes as he ran his knuckles over her cheek.

She ached in places she didn't know she had. Most of those had to do with the exertion of dragging heavy, leafed-out tree branches from the stream. Others, from their lovemaking.

Skimming the hard line of his jaw with her fingertips, amazed by her freedom to touch him, she smiled. "Never better."

The inviting curve of her mouth beckoned. If his daughter hadn't been due to wake up soon, he knew exactly where he would be leading this woman right now. He didn't trust the strength of the desire he felt, the blind power of it. But it was undeniably there. The need he felt for her might have been a lot more threatening, too, had he not been living in the moment with her. Only the moment. The way he knew she was doing with him.

"Glad to hear that," he murmured. She had her hair pulled into a low ponytail again. Smoothing his hand over her crown, he let it drift along its soft length.

"How about you?" she asked, her head down as she toyed with a button on his shirt.

"Just hungry. I need food," he told her, then dropped a quick kiss to the top of her head and turned to the refrigerator before he could further sidetrack himself.

"I can do that," he heard her say. "Fix your breakfast, I mean."

He knew she didn't have to meet Kate at the cookhouse for a while. Kate really didn't even need her help now that she was back to cooking for his core crew, but the women seemed to like working together. He was about to tell her she didn't need to fry his eggs, though, when the phone rang. Instead, he said, "Hang on," on his way to the desk and snatched up the receiver with his usual, "Carter."

He expected the call to be from Ty. His foreman would be leaving soon to make the hundred-mile drive to Miles City to pick up the alfalfa seed he'd ordered. Ty would be checking to see if there was anything else they needed from the larger town. Or it could be Ace, making the call for him. Ace would be tilling today. Kenny would ride fence. Wiley and Roy Dee would be working with the barn and stable animals and lubing the tractor.

He wasn't expecting Bree Mabry.

"No problem," he assured, when the older woman with the faintly accented voice apologized for calling at such an early hour. "A few more minutes and you'd have missed her." It surprised him how much she sounded like her niece, or her niece like her, as she thanked him. But, then, he'd never really talked to her much before. "She's right here."

Sophie wore one of his old chambray shirts open over a white Silver Spur pullover Kate had given her. In the process of finishing his coffee, she was pushing one rolled sleeve a little higher when he walked over with the portable phone.

"It's your aunt," he said, and watched her give him a puzzled little smile as she lifted the phone to her ear.

"Aunt Bree," he heard her say, as she slipped the carafe into place. "You're up early."

The call might not have been expected, but Carter thought little of it as he pulled out a skillet, then headed back to the fridge for the butter. He knew her aunt phoned with some regularity to visit with her. Though, mostly, he suspected, the calls were to check on her welfare. The welfare her husband had entrusted to him.

The disquiet that came with the thought had barely hit when he glanced toward Sophie. He hadn't been listening to what else she'd said. Not that she'd said much. But the ease in her manner had disappeared.

When he caught her eye, she immediately looked away and headed toward the table. The far end held the materials Kate had given her to help put together recipes for a community fundraiser. That was where she stopped.

Drawing a deep breath, Sophie rubbed between her eyes and slowly shook her head.

"When?" she asked, disappointment vying with disbelief.

"Two days," her aunt said.

"Don't call her yet. Please," she asked, speaking of her mother's secretary. The enormously efficient Lady Herzog-Biggs had been entrusted with making the arrangements to bring her home. Since Her Majesty's private jet was too large to land at the airstrip by the Mabrys, it would fly to San Francisco as it had before. Bree and Matt's smaller plane would come for her and return her there. "I'll call you back in a little while. Is that all right?"

Her aunt didn't miss much. Her immediate response was to ask what was wrong. Bree then reminded her that she'd called to tell her that her exile was over; that she no longer had to stay in a strange place with people she didn't really know. Even if she hadn't been thrilled by the prospect of returning home, her aunt said she'd have thought Sophie would at least sound relieved to be going back to civilization.

Unless, of course, she didn't want to leave.

Her mother's younger sister was nothing if not astute.

"That's a lot of it," Sophie quietly admitted. "I'll call you back."

She could feel Carter's eyes on her as she returned the phone to its base.

"What's going on?" he asked, coming up behind her.

As he had when he'd first come in, he curved his hand over her shoulder. It remained there as she turned to the concern carved in his face.

"I've been summoned back. The trade agreement has been signed." Disbelief at the timing caused the slow shake of her head. "A plane will be sent for me in two days."

She was nowhere near ready to leave. She needed more time. *They* needed more time. What had begun to build between them was far too rare to her for her to let go. After the way he started to share his life with her, after the way he'd kissed her just minutes ago, she wanted badly to know he wanted that time, too.

Something guarded shadowed his eyes as his thumb brushed the side of her neck. She felt tenderness in his touch, the amazing gentleness she'd come to discover beneath all his hard, honed strength.

"We knew this was coming," he said, sounding as if he was trying to deal with the suddenness of the news himself.

"I know." She'd just thought that the royal powers-that-be would want her out of sight a little longer after things had been resolved. "But I can ask to stay longer," she told him, encouraged by the way his hand had settled at the side of her neck. His thumb eased under her jaw, tracing it toward the corner of her mouth. "My grandmother and parents will spend the next few months at the summer castle in the mountains. Official functions come to a halt this time of year. They won't resume until September."

With nothing required of her in Valdovia, she'd much rather stay here. Carter could see that in her eyes. Part of him still wasn't ready for her to leave, either. He hadn't known how much longer they'd had. He hadn't let himself think about it. But another part, the stronger, more self-protective part, sensed reprieve beneath the sharp sense of disappointment.

The longer she stayed, the further under his skin she'd get—and things had already gone further than he'd ever intended. He'd made the mistake once of becoming involved with a woman he'd thought he had everything in common with, but who'd ultimately wanted only to change, then move beyond, his world. This woman—this princess—knew what existed beyond his world and could have just about anything in it—which was far more than he could give her when the novelty of his life wore off.

Far more important was her effect on his daughter. Hanna already adored her. The longer Sophie was around, the more attached his little girl would become.

The need to protect his child jerked hard.

"Postponing the inevitable will only make things worse. I don't want that," he insisted, his voice quiet. "For any of us. Especially for Hanna."

His hand eased away, fell to his side. "Your leaving won't be easy for her," he admitted, the regret in his tone there for a number of reasons. "You know she's not over her mother abandoning her. If you stay, it's only going to make it that much harder on her when you go. She doesn't need that. We have the next two days," he said, looking for a way to get them back to where they'd been before last night. "Let's just take them as they come."

We have two days…

The words sounded in her head like the slam of a door.

He didn't want her there. It didn't matter that she'd felt more complete with him than she'd ever felt with anyone. It didn't matter that he'd made her feel as if he really cared about her. It was as clear as the distance shadowing his face that the parts of his life he'd shared with her had meant far more to her than to him, and that what they'd shared last night meant next to nothing to him at all.

There were advantages to having learned to pretend. Though Sophie suddenly felt as hollow as a hole, she tried to make believe that what she'd heard was exactly what she'd expected. After all, she'd known all along how disillusioned his marriage had left him. She knew he had no desire for a relationship. Not the kind that involved his heart. If he ever did give in to commitment, to marriage, it would only be because he wanted to preserve his heritage. If it hadn't been for how much the realization hurt, she'd have found it ironic that he didn't see her as having any potential there, either.

Wounded to her core, trying not to look it, she tipped up her chin.

"Let's not," she replied, gamely. "I don't want a lot of awkwardness between us, Carter. I'll just go today. I'll call my aunt and tell her I want to stay at their lodge." The temporary caretakers were there. The Bauers were due tomorrow. Maybe she could help them. Even if she couldn't, at the very least, she'd have time to finish helping Kate with her recipe project. "I'll ask Kate to drop me off on her way to the Scotts with Hanna.

"And Hanna," she continued, hating how he'd made it sound as if she was abandoning her the way her mother had. "I won't go without telling her why I have to. She needs to know my leaving has nothing to do with her, so I'll explain that my mother has asked me to come home, and that my home is very far away. I'm also going to tell her I'll write her," she warned, not sure if it was his tension or hers knotting her stomach, "and that I'll send her a tutu and ballet slippers. I'd appreciate it if you'd give her the package when it arrives.

"And the horses," she continued, because they'd been her responsibility, "you'll take care of them until Mr. Bauer is better?"

Carter wasn't sure what to make of how calm she sounded. His experience with women was that breakups involved tears, accusations. At the very least, a little yelling was involved. Not that he wanted that. Not with his daughter in the house. And not that he thought Sophie would. She was too much of a lady for that.

It wasn't until he took a step closer that he noticed what his defensiveness had made him miss; the brightness in her eyes that totally belied her outward calm.

"Will you?" she pressed.

"Of course I will. Sophie, look," he said, thinking he'd rather have her yell at him than see her tears, "you knew you'd have to leave. You knew this was temporary."

She knew what he was doing. He was trying to shift the blame to her when he was the one pulling the plug on the relationship. But he was right. There had never been any question of her not returning home. What had happened between them, whatever it was that had grown over the past couple of weeks, simply had nowhere else to go.

Not without him allowing it.

And that clearly wasn't going to happen.

"What I know," she said, because he'd asked that she always be honest with him, "is that I'm not your ex-wife. I would never deliberately hurt your child." She really resented his implication that she had no regard for his daughter's feelings. *She doesn't need that,* he'd said, as if she had no concept of what his child struggled with. "I also know I need something from you. I need your word that last night…that you…that what…"

Her offense turned to something infinitely more discomfiting as she cut herself off and tried again. "Last night was—"

Something primitive in him refused to let her call it a mistake.

"Last night was strictly between us," he cut in, before the word could escape. "You won't find anything about us in the tabloids, Sophie." He started to tell her she should know that.

It occurred to him as his defenses continued to rise like thunderclouds over the mountains that he'd just given her reason not to assume anything about him at all.

Hating that, he held out his hand. "Not from me."

In her heart, Sophie knew that. She'd just needed to hear it.

She glanced at to his work-roughened hand, refusing thoughts of how gentle it could be. She considered only that his handshake was his word.

Needing that, too, she slipped her hand into his, felt his firm squeeze.

"Thank you," she whispered, and immediately pulled back, curling her fingers into her palm.

Carter's only response was to fist his hands on his hips, lower his head and blow a long, low breath. He was searching for something to say, she felt sure of it. Pretty sure it wasn't going to be anything she wanted to hear, she took a step back.

Hanna could walk in any minute.

"I need to talk to Kate" was all she could think to say herself, and she headed for the door.

Chapter Eleven

Carter couldn't ignore the high-pitched whine of the decelerating jet any longer.

He'd almost finished loading the back of his truck with sacks of alfalfa seed from outside the storage shed when he'd first noticed the sound. Having just hefted in the last two bags, he tipped back the brim of his Stetson and looked toward the clouds billowing like tufts of cotton in the sharp blue sky. The small white jet flew low, descending rapidly as it arced for the airstrip he shared with the Mabrys.

He didn't have to wonder whose it was, or whom it was for.

He hadn't seen Sophie since she'd walked out of his kitchen two days ago. He'd dropped off Hanna at the cookhouse as usual with her hairbrush and the barrettes she'd chosen for the day, but he hadn't gone in himself. He knew from Kate, though, that Sophie had helped with breakfast, then gone back to the house to collect her things before Kate had driven her the five miles to the Mabrys' place. His cook had clearly sensed something more going on other than what an apparently subdued Sophie had told her and his equally subdued daughter about having to end her holiday because of a family matter. The older woman had been wise enough not to press. She had expressed regret that she'd had to leave, though. The Mabrys' guest had seemed to become part of everything in no time and she thought it would feel kind of strange with her gone.

Wiley had told him the same thing when he'd mentioned her saying goodbye to him and the horses. His other men hadn't said much about her departure, other than that they'd miss her tarts, but he knew she'd said goodbye to them, too.

He could still see the quick stab of pain in her eyes when he hadn't asked her to stay, and her quick scramble for composure.

At the thought, he blew a long, self-recriminating breath. He hated what he'd done. He'd hated that he'd had to do it. But now as then and innumerable times in between, he told himself that what he'd felt with her was just a fluke— and that Hanna would get over her, too. Eventually.

Jerking down the brim of his hat, he headed for the driver's door of his truck. As Sophie had figured out, work was how he coped with what he didn't want to think about. Right now, he didn't want to think about the odd void in his gut. He had seed to sow and irrigation to set. Once the sound of that plane was gone, he was sure getting the lower hay field planted would be the only thing on his mind.

The small jet's powerful engines idled as Sophie fastened her seat belt. Within minutes of her uncle's plane landing, she'd been seated inside the jet's plush confines and the copilot had stowed her luggage. He'd just retracted the steps in preparation for turnaround and takeoff.

Outside the small window beside her, she could see Jenny Bauer's red SUV heading back toward her aunt and uncle's beautifully appointed lodge. The Bauers had proved to be exactly as her Aunt Bree and Kate had described them; good, conscientious people who took care of the Mabrys' property as if it were their own. The Clays, who would stay on until Dave could resume his chores, were new to caretaking, but seemed just as accommodating. The afternoon of Sophie's arrival, Mrs. Clay had asked if she'd like to go into town with her since she had to get groceries. Knowing she'd be leaving soon, wanting to see the town Kate had told her so much about and desperate for something to do to avoid thoughts of the man who didn't want her, Sophie had gone—only to encounter a tabloid at the market's checkout counter with a quarter-page photograph of herself under the caption *Princess Sophia Silenced?* The larger photos on the page had been of the cellulite on an American actress's bikini-clad bum.

It had only taken seconds of tsking about the exploitation of a little body fat for Mrs. Clay to shift her attention to the smaller photo, and for her to realize that the guest who'd been identified to her only as a Mabry niece was that 'missing' princess. She'd discreetly said nothing, however. If she wanted to stay employed by the Mabrys, what she knew of their guests needed to remain private. She hadn't even bought the tabloid, though she'd clearly been itching to do just that.

Thoughts of what Sophie might be returning to now collided with the awful ache in her chest as she watched the SUV disappear. Even with the plane's door now closed and secured, the engines whining, she hoped against hope that

Carter would appear and tell her he wanted her to stay; that he knew they needed more time together, too.

As if the thought had conjured the vehicle, a truck bounced onto the short road from the highway. But even as her pulse skipped, her hopes fell.

The truck wasn't Carter's.

There had been several customers in the store when she had gone with Mrs. Clay. Any one of them could have recognized her from the photograph. Apparently, the tentacled branches of the local grapevine had worked their way to the media. Within seconds of slamming the truck to a halt, the man driving it lifted a camera with a long, tea-saucer-sized lens to his face.

Sophie leaned back, completely out of view.

Her family would be proud. She had escaped the press and the paparazzi. No incriminating, embarrassing or otherwise inappropriate photographs would appear because of anything she had done.

All that little feat had cost her was her heart.

Try as she might, though, she couldn't make herself wish she'd never met the big, hard-driving, hard-headed rancher. Because of him, she now knew the difference between being protected and being controlled. The difference between going through life and actually having one. She knew how it felt to be useful and necessary, though she'd probably only been that way to Kate and Wiley, and then only for a little while. Because of Carter, she would also now never, ever trust her judgment about a man again, but that was just the price she had to pay for finally realizing nothing in her life would change unless she changed it herself.

She loved her family, the whole pretentious, probably dysfunctional lot of them, but she was tired of being the princess who tried so hard not to make a mistake only to have those she did make undermine her in the eyes of those she'd always tried to please. She was even more tired of being the royal substitute, the princess whose main contribution was filling in for someone else.

As agitated as she felt, she might even have told her mother that, had her mother not already left for the summer castle in the mountains by the time Sophie arrived at the main palace in the small country's capital. The queen and the other members of the royal family, along with their personal staffs, had departed for the summer, too. Apparently, the press's interest in her in Valdovia and Europe had waned after the announcement of the trade agreement's signing. Except for a couple of U.S. tabloids who'd picked up the story late, she was last week's news.

Which meant she was no longer of concern to the Crown.

That blessed reprieve made it easy for her to hole up at the palace by herself because she didn't feel like fit company for anyone, anyway. It was just her and the roughly fifty remaining members of the household staff whose jobs were to tend the gardens, the grounds, the livery, the housekeeping and the ritual summer cleaning of the carpets and draperies. Even with so many people around, she saw few of them. But the atmosphere without the Queen and the Princess Royal in residence was far more relaxed than when they were. Not to the point where protocol was forgotten. That would never happen. When Aldrich, the butler she'd last seen polishing a chandelier in a downstairs hall appeared with his jacket properly buttoned over his vest and announced that Princess Brianna's guest had arrived, he was every bit as formal and proper as he would have been had he been addressing the queen herself.

"Princess Brianna's guest?" Sophie asked, looking up from

her lists. Her Aunt Bree had given up her place in line to the throne when she'd married Matthew years ago, but she still retained her title and all the deference that came with it. "Is Aunt Brianna here?"

Sophie rose from the table in the plant-filled sunroom. Nearly covering the table's mosaic tiles were her ever-expanding lists. Lists of tack and equipment needed for dressage, for steeple chase, for a stable, and for the barrel racing Wiley had told her about.

Bree hadn't said a word about coming for a visit. All they'd talked about in the two weeks since Sophie had left Montana were Sophie's plan for an identity of her own, which Bree fully supported, and the meteoric rise and fall of her relationship with Carter. Her aunt lived her life following the dictates of her own heart, so she'd immediately recognized why Sophie had suddenly been in such a hurry to leave his ranch when she'd first so clearly wanted to stay. Her aunt now knew about her and Matthew's friend; that she'd fallen in love with him, anyway. And with his little girl. Since Bree now had a guest waiting for her, she must have thought her niece needed the boost of more personal support, and arranged to meet a friend as long as she was here.

Or, so Sophie was thinking as she prepared to greet her by smoothing the white slacks she wore with the soft yellow sweater she'd thrown on to boost her mood.

"No, Your Highness," the gray-haired butler replied. "She isn't here. Just the gentleman she called about. I've escorted Mr. McLeod to the east drawing room.

"Is there a problem, ma'am?" he asked, when she went as still as the statues in the garden. "Your aunt said he's a personal friend here on holiday, and that you'd give him a tour of the gardens. She called just a while ago so I could alert the guard at the gate. I thought you expected him. If I misunderstood…"

"No. No, you didn't misunderstand," she assured the man who appeared fully prepared to beg her forgiveness. "I just…forgot." Hoping the excuse didn't sound as lame as it was, she gave him a reassuring smile. "Please tell him I'm on my way."

Clearly relieved, the older gentleman offered a bow and left her staring after him in disbelief. Partly at what her aunt had done. Mostly that Carter was actually there.

"Her Highness will be here shortly," said a very proper male voice from the doorway. "Please, sir. Do have a seat."

The slight but sharp-eyed butler who'd met Carter at the palace's high, gilded and carved front doors, surreptitiously glanced from the six-foot, four-inch length of his decidedly large frame to the delicate three-legged table three feet from him. Atop the table rested a two-foot high, probably irreplaceable, definitely breakable porcelain figurine of a woman on a swing with hundreds of tiny porcelain roses twined around it.

"Thanks," Carter said, giving that same skeptical glance to the spindly legs of the ornate chairs and oval-backed sofas in the painting-filled room. Despite the urban chic he'd yet to eradicate from his kitchen, he was accustomed to dark, polished woods and overstuffed leather. Everything in this room looked pastel, gilded, brocaded and decidedly antique. "But I'm more comfortable standing."

The guy looked as if he was afraid he'd say that. "I understand," he conceded.

With a deferential nod, he departed, closing the room's double doors once more.

Her Highness.

Carter remembered having used the title in his head a couple of times. Yet, until the taxi he'd taken from his hotel had to be cleared by a uniformed guard at the palace's massive gates and he'd followed a road cut through lawns that could have grazed fifty head of cattle, then been escorted through an ornately decorated foyer so vast his boots echoed on the tiled floor, the reality of what Sophie lived with simply hadn't sunk in.

Even the pictures he'd seen of the place on the Internet and Matt's admission about how the place had "sort of" intimidated him when he'd first seen it hadn't fully prepared him. He wasn't ready, either, for the sight of her when one of the doors opened again and she stepped inside.

He couldn't believe how much he'd missed her.

She looked like a ray of sunshine in buttercup yellow and sleek white. Her shining dark hair was clipped back from her face, much as she'd always worn it. Topaz and silver earrings dangled from her ears.

She didn't look at him as she closed the door. Not until she leaned against it with both hands behind her, still holding the latch, did her gold-flecked brown eyes meet his.

Totally wary, filled with hope she didn't dare trust and trying not to let either show, Sophie schooled her features into an unreadable mask. Carter stood halfway across the room, his size and his formidable presence dominating the space as powerfully as any ambassador or president ever to be greeted there.

The dark hair combed back from his freshly shaved face no longer curled over his collar. Neatly trimmed now, it merely brushed it. Denim and chambray had been replaced by a beautiful black suit and collarless shirt that turned his gray eyes nearly silver. It also looked suspiciously designer. Not elegant Italian. More aggressively confident American.

His shiny black boots looked new.

A warrior in Ralph Lauren and cowboy boots.

"Where's Hanna?" she asked.

"She's with Kate." Carter wasn't sure which had surprised the woman more; that Sophie was the princess she'd seen in some tabloid, or that he was going after her. "By the way, she's practically living in her tutu," he told her, sounding far more at ease than he felt. "And she misses you. A lot."

Sophie didn't know what she was supposed to say to that. A faint smile formed, knowing her gift had been received and enjoyed, but it wasn't her fault that she wasn't there for the child she missed terribly herself.

The smile gave way to caution. "Why are you here?"

His shoulders rose with his deep breath a moment before he jammed his hands onto his hips. The stance was familiar, an automatic response to everything from frustration to contemplation. It also made him bigger. The way he dropped his arms and glanced at the intricate urns on the ornamental tables made it apparent he knew that.

"Can we go for a walk or something? I'm afraid to move in here."

Her aunt had said something about giving "her guest" a tour of the gardens. The excuse she'd used to get him into the palace seemed like a lovely idea, though. Being outside was infinitely preferable to standing there with his tension bouncing off the drawing room's plastered walls.

She felt like pacing herself.

Rather than opening the doors behind her, she crossed to the French doors beyond a seventeenth-century writing desk. They opened to a wide stone-arched and columned breezeway lined with square pots of rounded orange trees. On either side stretched lawns, gardens, fountains.

"Better?" she asked, her flats tapping lightly on the travertine tiles.

"Much," he said, falling into step beside her.

The early summer sun warmed the air. The faint breeze passing through the long colonnade carried the scent of the blooming roses. "You were about to explain what brings you here."

At the reminder, Carter reached to tug down the brim of his hat, only to remember he wasn't wearing it. He felt a little naked being outdoors in the daytime without it, too. He'd have brought his dress hat, the eight-hundred-dollar Stetson he usually only wore to weddings and funerals, but he hadn't thought it would be appropriate in the midst of so much formality. She'd made concessions living in his world. He needed her to know that he was willing to make them when he was in hers.

Aside from that, he hadn't wanted to draw any particular attention to himself with whoever he ran into here. That was why he'd asked Mabry what a guy wore to meet a princess.

"You've probably already figured out that I've talked to Matt."

"Since it was my aunt who got you in here," she replied, her focus on the view where the colonnade ended a hundred feet away. "I thought you must have talked to her."

"I did that, too," he murmured. "Matt figured I should talk to her after I asked him how a person goes about getting into a place like this. I didn't think I could just show up at the gate.

"I didn't want to chance you not seeing me," he continued, pushing his hands into his pockets as they continued on. As badly as he wanted to touch her, he wasn't certain how welcome his touch would be. "So I asked her if she'd mind just arranging it and not saying anything to you. She was okay with that after I told her what I wanted."

Giving him nothing, Sophie glanced toward him. Waiting.

He could hardly blame her caution. When she'd told him what she wanted—just to stay with him a while longer—he'd shot her down in flames.

"While we were talking," he prefaced, needing to ease into it, "Bree mentioned the proposal you're preparing for your grandmother. For the riding school."

He clearly remembered the day in his stables when Sophie had told him how she would love to work with children and horses, and how that avenue was closed to her because her more accomplished older sister oversaw the Queen's riding program. The plan Sophie had come up with wouldn't compete with that. She'd told her aunt she would work with the kids who weren't considered competition material; kids who just loved being around horses. Or kids who might not have a chance to know they loved them without someone giving them the opportunity.

"She thinks it's a long shot," he said.

"I know she does. But I have to try." Sophie couldn't imagine what his interest in her little project could be. She just knew she needed desperately to focus on what she loved, the way he did with his ranch and his daughter. "If the Crown won't approve it under its auspices, I'll tell my grandmother I'll open it as my own charity."

Bree had mentioned that, too. "How will that go over?"

"Probably not well."

Since the Crown's failure to endorse one of their own would undoubtedly earn a headline or two, her grandmother might reconsider—right after she'd picked up her royal dentures from the floor. Sophie had never in her life challenged authority. But as great a sense of responsibility and duty as she'd been taught to feel toward her family, it seemed to her they had a few responsibilities and duties toward her, too.

"I'm only doing what you suggested," she quietly informed him. "You said 'start your own,' so that's what I'll do." That day in his stables, he'd made his easy solution sound as if she was the only one holding herself back. Realizing now that she also had a duty to herself, she knew he'd been right. "I'm going after what I want.

"I know I can do this," she insisted, conscious of him glancing toward her as they walked. There were other things she wanted, too. But bucking the Crown seemed easier somehow than thinking about how badly she wanted him in her life. Having given him her heart only to have it handed back to her, she wasn't about to tell him that.

"I know you can, Sophie. And you'll be great at it." Carter felt the tension in his shoulders work its way to his jaw. He looked toward her, then back to the elaborate fountain visible in the arched opening ahead of them. "I just wondered if you think you could get Hanna on a horse."

Beside him, she came to a stop.

Confusion swept the delicate lines of her face. "Here?"

"Here. Or there," he said, but he was getting ahead of himself.

Lifting his hand, he pushed his fingers through his hair. He wished he was better at this, but he was going with his gut with her. Since this was uncharted territory for him, his gut instincts were all he had.

"I don't want to let you go," he finally admitted. "At least not before I let you know that what happened between us wasn't one-sided. The feelings, I mean."

He knew she never would have made love with him if her heart hadn't been involved. That was the thought he clung to as he watched her go still. He hadn't known what to make of all he'd felt for her, what he'd felt *with* her. He did now, though. Just as he knew that she'd become a part of him somehow. And that a huge void existed in his life without her.

For so long, he'd lived season to season, not looking beyond the next and just looking forward to the day being over. She'd shown him how to take pleasure in the moments, and reminded him of how good life could be when that pleasure wasn't missing.

"The whole time you were there, I wanted to believe I was protecting Hanna by limiting her time with you," he confessed, though he was certain she already knew that. "And I wanted to believe I was protecting her when I didn't ask you to stay. But I was protecting myself, too. Like you protected yourself," he added in his defense.

She frowned up at him. "Excuse me?"

"Come on, Sophie." She should understand where he'd been coming from. She'd been there herself. Still was for all he knew. "You'd resigned yourself to the idea of a loveless marriage rather than risk trusting the wrong person. You of all people know how hard it is to let your heart get mixed up in a relationship."

She didn't look at all willing to be that understanding of him just then. "If I'd been protecting myself all that well, I never would have fallen in love…" *With you.*

His eyes narrowed on hers. "What did you say?"

Looking as if she'd already said far more than she'd intended, her focus fell to the veins in the travertine between their feet. "You heard me."

Encouraged enormously by her almost-admission, he tipped up her chin with his fingers. She wasn't going to risk any more of herself until he'd laid himself on the line. Needing her trust back, he could do nothing less.

"I love you," he said simply. "And you don't have to live in a loveless marriage. I love you, Sophie. You. Not the princess, the granddaughter of a queen and whoever all else it is you're related to. I can't offer you a castle or a title, other than Mrs. McLeod, but I can give you a good life—if that's the life you want. Life on the ranch suited you, didn't it?"

With his thumb grazing her cheek, she gave him a stunned little nod. Or maybe what he'd sensed was hesitation.

"I'm not asking you to give up what's important to you here," he assured her. He now knew how love was supposed to feel. When people loved each other, they wanted to compromise, to make things work. Love wasn't about asking the other person to choose. "I wouldn't be able to leave from calving to fall roundup. The slowest times of the year here are the busiest times of the year on the ranch," he reminded her, "but we can come back off and on in the winter. Ty can manage things fine while we're gone. And summers at the ranch, you can bring kids in for your riding school."

The way her hand had just curved over his wrist relieved him enormously. So did the warmth battling the disbelief in her eyes. He just wished she'd say something.

Feeling the need to strengthen his case, anyway, he covered the last of his bases.

"I understand from your uncle that royals marrying outside their ranks is becoming more common all the time. There's something about a non-royal signing papers acknowledging no right to royal assets," he acknowledged, grateful for Matt's crash course in protocol. "And I guess I also need a member of the family to vouch for me," he said, wanting her to know he'd done his homework. "But Bree said she'd do it." If her niece still wanted him, she'd qualified.

"So how about it, Sophie?"

The hope she hadn't wanted to trust had broken past all her efforts to restrain it. He'd sort of lost her after he'd said he loved her, but she was pretty sure she'd caught the gist of everything else.

It sounded as if he was offering her everything she could ever want.

She just need to be sure.

"How about what?" she asked, her heart hammering.

Carter had known all along that he was bound to forget something. It occurred to him as he drew back and slipped his hand into his inside jacket pocket for the ring he hadn't known for sure she'd accept, that he hadn't actually proposed.

The small loop of platinum and diamonds seemed tiny in his big hand. Bree had suggested he keep the style simple. Sophie wasn't a flashy sort of woman.

Holding it between his thumb and index finger, knowing this woman held his future in her hands, he met her eyes.

"I have two questions, Sophie." He'd buried his dreams of a life with someone he cared about, who cared about him, his daughter and his ranch. But she'd crashed through his defenses as if they'd been as insubstantial as glass, and resurrected those dreams all over again. "Will you marry me? Will you be Hanna's mom?"

Sophie's heart felt as if it was about to burst as she held his quicksilver eyes. "You know, Carter," she murmured, "I can't think of anything I want more."

"Nothing?" he asked, slipping the exquisite ring on her finger.

"Nothing," she repeated, rising on tiptoe to slip her arms around his neck. "Except those sons you want to carry on your dad's legacy."

His arms were already around her, gathering her closer to the hard length of his body. As if hungry for details he might have forgotten, his eyes roamed her face moments before one corner of his mouth kicked up.

He drew her closer still, something deliciously heated in his eyes. "We'll talk about that later," he assured her, and covered her mouth with his.

The thought of her having his baby added a whole new dimension to a kiss filled with relief to simply be holding her again, and with promise and hope, longing and need. Together they had a shot at preserving his legacy. But even more important than that, he and Hanna would share their lives with the woman who'd taught him the importance of experiencing the moments. From now on, it was all about enjoying the journey.

With his princess for a wife, he'd definitely enjoy the ride.

Epilogue

For Sophie, summer and early fall had passed in a blur of transatlantic flights, packing, moving and cooking for the men who'd come back for fall roundup. Her and Carter's wedding in July had been decidedly small and sudden, by royal standards, anyway. Neither of them had wanted to wait the traditional six months after an official announcement of their engagement to wed. They hadn't wanted any of the pomp and circumstance that would only have complicated the event, either, so they had opted for a quiet ceremony in the chapel of the palace. Her royal grandmother had ultimately bestowed her blessings on them both—and on the little girl who had charmed them all that day. Hanna, in a white ballerina-length flower-girl dress, had looked like a little princess herself as she'd stood with them before the ornate altar. When the priest had asked Carter if he took Sophia Victoria Mathilde as his wedded wife, Hanna had looked up at her dad and quietly added, "and my mom."

Behind her, Sophie could hear the little girl who'd completely stolen her heart talking to her puppy in the mudroom. The giggle in Hanna's small voice made her smile. So did the sight of Carter as he climbed from his truck and his powerful, long-legged strides carried him toward the house. Behind him, the sunset glowed orange on the horizon, its blaze of color as spectacular as the golds and rusts of the aspens and poplars in the windbreak.

Fall roundup was finally over. The last of the seasonal help had packed up, after a night of celebrating in Eagle Prairie, and moved on last week. After the work of shipping stock off to market and moving the breeding stock to their winter range, the days had become almost…peaceful.

Carter tipped back the brim of his Stetson, his boots thudding on the wooden steps.

Looking as if he rather liked the idea of finding her there, he dipped his head toward hers. "Were you waiting for me?" he asked, curving his arm around her waist.

With a smile in her eyes, she looped her arms around his neck and met his quick kiss. "Sorry," she murmured, "but no." Easing closer, loving how free she was to touch him, she splayed her hand over his broad, flannel-covered chest. "After you called to say you were on your way, I thought I'd just come out and watch the sun set. Dinner needs a little longer in the oven, anyway. You had nothing to do with it."

He clearly wasn't buying her sass. "You were waiting for me," he concluded, and drew her up to kiss away her grin as the back door popped open.

"Hi, Daddy!" Hanna's quick smile collapsed. "Riley, no!"

Carter groaned as the small mass of black-and-white fur streaked ahead of his little girl. Hanna darted down the stairs after him, the long end of her neat French braid flying.

She'd dressed her dog again. Accessorized it, anyway. A row of little silver butterfly clips held the hair on his head up in little tufts. The sparkly pink ribbon around his neck had been tied into a bow. In self-defense, the enterprising canine had one of the bow's trailing ends in his mouth, effectively untying it as he shook his head hard enough to send one of the clips flying. Preoccupied with losing the bow, he'd slowed down enough for Hanna to scoop him into her arms and plop down with him in the pile of leaves that had drifted from a cottonwood tree.

"Does she have to dress him like that?"

"Little girls like to dress things up," came Sophie's easy reply. "That's one of the reasons they play with dolls. It's a mothering instinct," she added, clearly trying not to laugh when he frowned. "It's what little girls do."

He had to trust her on that. He was still bumping around in the dark when it came to what his daughter liked. But he had no problem relying on the woman who'd seemed to understand Hanna pretty much the instant she'd met her. He'd never thought he'd see his daughter so happy, or so totally at ease with anything on four legs. The puppy wriggling in her lap had started out tiny a few months ago, but had to be pushing twenty pounds now. Grown, he'd top out in the sixty-pound range.

Carter had Sophie to thank for what he was seeing, his daughter giggling and falling onto her back as the exuberant baby border collie licked her cheek. Sophie had brought the pup up from the barn after learning that the rest of the litter refused to let him nurse. She'd made no attempt to have Hanna help, though. She'd simply let her work her way on her own from gingerly petting the little guy to helping bottle-feed him. Now, with the bottle long gone and Riley sharing her bed, the once animal-skittish child didn't seem to notice—or care—how big he was getting.

As the sunset flamed gold, orange and pink beyond where his daughter played, he drew Sophie in front of him.

Catching his arm where it rested across her shoulder blades, she seemed to be taking in what he saw, too. "You were right, Carter," he heard her murmur. "You said I'd love autumn here."

The contentment in her voice humbled him. She could have lived in a palace, worn the crown jewels, had servants at her beck and call. Instead she'd found what she needed here, dressed in denim and fleece to ward off the deepening chill and loving something he'd forgotten to notice.

"You know something else?" she asked.

He kissed the top of her head, feeling richer than any king. "What?"

"She'll make a great big sister."

Her contentment seemed to wash over him as he slipped his hand over the slight bulge of her belly. They'd talked about waiting a year to expand their family. He hadn't wanted to rush her. He'd wanted to give her time to establish herself in this place. But she'd insisted she wanted nothing more than to have his child. She'd said it could be his wedding present to her.

So he'd given her what she—they—wanted.

As his daughter ran back into the house with her puppy hot on her heels, he turned his princess in his arms, holding her to his heart. She'd said she loved autumn. Because of her, he was now looking forward to all the seasons. But what he looked forward to most just then were the once endlessly long and cold winter nights—and sharing them all with her.

* * * * *

*Celebrate 60 years of pure reading pleasure with
Harlequin®!*

*Step back in time and enjoy a sneak preview of an exciting
anthology from Harlequin® Historical with*
THE DIAMONDS OF WELBOURNE MANOR

This compelling anthology features three stories about
the outragcous Fitzmanning sisters. Meet Annalise, who
is never at a loss for words… But that can change with
an unexpected encounter in the forest.

Available May 2009 from Harlequin® Historical.

"I'm the illegitimate daughter of notoriously scandalous parents, Mr. Milford. Candidates for my hand are unlikely to be lining up at the gates."

"Don't be so quick to discount your charms, my dear. Or the charm of your substantial dowry. Or even your brothers' influence. There are as many reasons to marry as there are marriages."

Annalise snorted. "Oh, yes. Perhaps I shall marry for dynastic reasons, or perhaps for property or influence. After all, a loveless, practical marriage worked out so well for my mother."

"Well, you've routed me on that one. I can think of no suitable rejoinder." Ned rose to his feet and extended his hand. "And since that is the case, let me be the first to wish you a long and happy spinsterhood."

Her mouth gaped open. And then she laughed.

And he froze.

This was the first time, Ned realized. The first time he'd seen her eyes light up and her mouth curl. The first time he'd witnessed her features melded together in glorious accord to produce exquisite beauty.

Unbelievable what a change came over her face. Unheard of what effect her throaty, rasping laughter had on his body. It pounded a beat upon his ear, quickly taken up by his pulse. It echoed through him, finally residing in his stirring nether regions.

So easily she did it, awakened these sensations within him—without any apparent effort at all. And she had called him potentially dangerous? Clearly the intelligent thing for him to do would be to steer clear, to leave her to the tender ministrations of Lord Peter Blackthorne.

"You were right." She smiled up at him as she took his hand and climbed to her feet. "I do feel better."

Ah, well. When had he ever chosen the intelligent path?

He did not relinquish her hand. He used it to pull her in, close enough that he could feel the warmth of her. "At the risk of repeating Lord Peter's mistake and anticipating too much—may I ask if you'll be my partner in battledore tomorrow?"

Her smiled dimmed. Her breath came a little faster. His own had gone shallow, as if he'd just run a race—and lost. He ran his gaze over the appealing lift of her brow and the curious angle of her chin. His index finger twitched.

"I should like that," she said.

His finger trembled again and he lifted it, traced the pink and tender shell of her ear, the unique sweep of her jaw. Her pulse leaped beneath her skin, triggering his own. Slowly he tilted her chin up, waiting for her to object, to step back, to slap his hand away.

She did none of those eminently sensible things. Which left him free to do the entirely impractical thing.

Baby soft, the skin of her lips. Her whole body trembled when he touched her there.

He leaned in. Her eyes closed, even as she stood straight against him, strung as tight as a bow. He pressed his mouth to hers. It was a soft kiss, sweet and chaste. And yet he was hot and hard and as ready as he'd ever been in his life.

She drew back a little. Sighed. Their breath mingled a moment before she slowly backed away.

"Oh," she breathed. Her dark eyes were full of wonder and something that looked like fear. He took a step toward her, but she only shook her head. His outstretched hand fell to his side as she turned to disappear into the wood. This was the first time, Ned realized. The first time, since he'd come to the house party at Welbourne Manor, that he'd seen her eyes light up.

* * * * *

Follow Ned and Annalise's story in May 2009 in
THE DIAMONDS OF WELBOURNE MANOR
Available May 2009 from Harlequin® Historical

Available in the series romance section, or in the historical romance section, wherever books are sold.

We'll be spotlighting a different series every month throughout 2009 to celebrate our 60th anniversary.

Look for Harlequin® Historical in May!

Celebrations begin with
a sumptuous Regency house party!

Join three scandalous sisters in

**THE DIAMONDS OF
WELBOURNE MANOR**

Glittering, scintillating, sensual fun
by Diane Gaston, Deb Marlowe
and Amanda McCabe.

**60 years of Harlequin,
600 years of romance
in Harlequin Historical!**

www.eHarlequin.com

HHBPA09

HARLEQUIN®

American ★ Romance®

LAURA MARIE ALTOM
The Marine's Babies

Men Made in America

Captain Jace Monroe is everything a Marine should be—strong, brave and honorable. He's also an instant father of twin baby girls he never knew existed! Life gets even more complicated when he finds himself attracted to Emma Stewart, his new nanny. But can this sexy, fun-loving bachelor do the right thing and become a family man? Emma and the babies are counting on it!

**Available in May
wherever books are sold.**

LOVE, HOME & HAPPINESS

www.eHarlequin.com   HAR75261

REQUEST YOUR FREE BOOKS!

2 FREE NOVELS PLUS 2 FREE GIFTS!

SPECIAL EDITION®

Life, Love and Family!

YES! Please send me 2 FREE Silhouette Special Edition® novels and my 2 FREE gifts (gifts are worth about $10). After receiving them, if I don't wish to receive any more books, I can return the shipping statement marked "cancel." If I don't cancel, I will receive 6 brand-new novels every month and be billed just $4.24 per book in the U.S. or $4.99 per book in Canada. That's a savings of at least 15% off the cover price! It's quite a bargain! Shipping and handling is just 25¢ per book*. I understand that accepting the 2 free books and gifts places me under no obligation to buy anything. I can always return a shipment and cancel at any time. Even if I never buy another book from Silhouette, the two free books and gifts are mine to keep forever.

235 SDN EEYU   335 SDN EEY6

Name _____ (PLEASE PRINT) _____

Address _____ Apt. # _____

City _____ State/Prov. _____ Zip/Postal Code _____

Signature (if under 18, a parent or guardian must sign)

Mail to the **Silhouette Reader Service:**
IN U.S.A.: P.O. Box 1867, Buffalo, NY 14240-1867
IN CANADA: P.O. Box 609, Fort Erie, Ontario L2A 5X3

Not valid to current subscribers of Silhouette Special Edition books.

Want to try two free books from another line?
Call 1-800-873-8635 or visit www.morefreebooks.com.

* Terms and prices subject to change without notice. Prices do not include applicable taxes. Sales tax applicable in N.Y. Canadian residents will be charged applicable provincial taxes and GST. Offer not valid in Quebec. This offer is limited to one order per household. All orders subject to approval. Credit or debit balances in a customer's account(s) may be offset by any other outstanding balance owed by or to the customer. Please allow 4 to 6 weeks for delivery. Offer available while quantities last.

Your Privacy: Silhouette is committed to protecting your privacy. Our Privacy Policy is available online at www.eHarlequin.com or upon request from the Reader Service. From time to time we make our lists of customers available to reputable third parties who may have a product or service of interest to you. If you would prefer we not share your name and address, please check here. ☐

SSE09

You're invited to join our Tell Harlequin Reader Panel!

By joining our new reader panel you will:

- Receive Harlequin® books—they are FREE and yours to keep with no obligation to purchase anything!
- Participate in fun online surveys
- Exchange opinions and ideas with women just like you
- Have a say in our new book ideas and help us publish the best in women's fiction

In addition, you will have a chance to win great prizes and receive special gifts! See Web site for details. Some conditions apply. Space is limited.

To join, visit us at
www.TellHarlequin.com.

Silhouette®

COMING NEXT MONTH

Available April 28, 2009